POPE JOAN

Lawrence Durrell

POPE JOAN

*translated and adapted from the Greek of
Emmanuel Royidis*

THE OVERLOOK PRESS

New York

First published by Tusk/Overlook in 1984 by

The Overlook Press
Lewis Hollow Road
Woodstock, New York 12498

Copyright © 1966 by Lawrence Durrell

Library of Congress Cataloging in Publication Data

Rhodés, Emmanouél D., 1835-1904.
  Pope Joan

  Translation of: Hé Papissa Ióanna.
  1. Joan (Legendary Pope)—Fiction.   I. Durrell,
Lawrence.   II. Title.
PA5610.R52P313   1984   889'.32   84-7116
ISBN 0-87951-963-0
ISBN 0-87951-964-9 (pbk)

If you would like a hardcover edition of this work for your
permanent library, spine bound in cloth and printed on 50lb.
Warren Sebago Cream White stock, please write to The Overlook
Press, Lewis Hollow Road, Woodstock, New York, 12498.

Third Printing

to

GEORGE KATSIMBALIS

Preface

THE LITERATURE OF modern Greece, which hitherto has been completely unknown to western readers, is now beginning to be explored in some detail. Novels like *Zorba* and *Aeolia* have enabled one to judge how lively is the prose tradition of this comparatively young country, while the names of poets like Cavafy and Seferis have begun to occupy their rightful place in the European tradition to which they have contributed and from which they spring.

Pope Joan has a double claim on our attention for it occupies a central position among the popular books of modern Greece; and it is also in its own way a small masterpiece which might occupy a position on the bookshelf of the discerning reader midway, say, between *Candide* and *Thaïs*. It is a masterpiece of irreverence, witty and a trifle improper in parts; but it is a very genuine example of a Mediterranean book, and in the hands of Royidis the character of Joanna becomes something more than a satirical puppet—a stick with which to beat the clericals. Indeed Pope Joan is a sort of brief record of the history and misfortunes of Eros after his transformation by Christianity from a God to an underground resistance-movement.

Papissa Joanna, as the book is called in Greek, sets out to trace the history of the mysterious Pope John VIII who for two years, five months and four days ruled Christendom from the seat of the Supreme Pontiff. Its author, Emmanuel Royidis, was born in 1835 and died in Athens towards the end of 1904. There seems little doubt that the romance was begun as a satire of affairs; but there is even less doubt that midway through the book Royidis found himself head over heels in love with his heroine, for he treats her with a sympathetic irony and tenderness which brings her very clearly to life.

Papissa Joanna first saw printer's ink and paper in 1886. The book's first appearance created a sensation. The authorities of the Orthodox Church were horrified by what seemed to them to be the impious irony of its author—and no less by the gallery of maggot-ridden church fathers which he described so lovingly. Royidis was excommunicated and his book banned. Despite the official prohibition, however, the book swept him to fame in Athens, while translations into other European languages brought him a certain degree of domestic respect among critics. The French edition alone sold several hundred thousand copies. The contrast is instructive, for the French Catholic press refused to rise to the elaborate tease and gave the book a smiling welcome for its very real literary qualities; realizing, one supposes, that the historic Joanna (if she ever existed) had long since joined all the other figures of church folklore and that literary squibs like these were hardly likely to disturb any serious faith worth the name. The Orthodox Church however remained extremely touchy on the envenomed subject of the she-Pope and after Royidis' death his fame seems to have suffered an eclipse in Greece, and it was only in 1920 that an edition of *Papissa Joanna* reappeared in Athens. It has sold steadily ever since, and at the time of writing its author's fame is secure in the history of modern Greek literature.

Royidis accepted his excommunication and Joanna's with philosophical indifference; as a good republican and anti-clerical he no doubt felt that he had managed to hole the enemy below the waterline. The odd thing is that while his book is the lightest and deftest of romances—a mere soufflé of a novel—it is based upon a profound knowledge not only of the period in which Pope Joan lived but also of the tangled mass of documentation upon which the case for her real existence rests. The author's preface to the definitive edition of Pope Joan consists of a lengthy review of those authorities which mentioned the she-Pope, and a considered assessment of the various claims for and against her existence. You would think that all this had little enough to do with the romance, but Royidis defended himself against his critics by asserting that he had invented very little for which some authority could not be found, and that his picture of Athens in the ninth century was derived from unimpeachable sources.

He reminded his critics with some asperity that the work contained only 'facts and events proved beyond discussion' and added for good measure: 'vague and ill-founded protests on behalf of morality will not only be meaningless but will remind us of the English poet's phrase: "Only the immoral talk of morals".'

So much for the professed intentions of the author; and so much for his sources. But when both have been established it remains to be said that the character of Joanna rides far above the circumscribed literary or sociological preoccupations of her creator. Like all good characters, she gives the impression of having been created rather than invented, and there is something touching about the innocence which is her only weapon against the real world with its bigotries and penalties.

Of Royidis himself a good deal has been made known; born to a modest patrimony he travelled much, and studied in France and Germany. A republican, he was naturally an Anglophile and read English for his own pleasure and instruction. In middle years he had to contend with money troubles, and during the tenure of Tricoupis as Prime Minister was several times appointed as Librarian to the Athens Library, only to be dislodged by the incoming Royalist faction.

His later years he spent in poverty—yet his stocky bearded figure was familiar to all who frequented the little taverns and eating-houses of the Athenian Plaka. Increasing deafness gave his features the expression of an urbanity and detachment which very well suited the creator of Joanna.

As an essayist and pamphleteer he was well known to the Athenian public, but it is doubtful whether any of his work in this field would justify translation. He was a man of one book—and having written it he was often called upon to defend it. This he did with great wit, irony and charm. Deaf to literary criticism as such, he was far more sensitive to the suggestion that Pope Joan was a purely apocryphal figure. He insisted to the last that he had invented little of the original story, and his pamphlet on the evidence for the existence of Pope Joan let loose all the pent-up flood-waters of rhetoric and scholarship with which he did not care to mar the romance. For Royidis was in love with Joanna, and could not bear to see her treated as a ninth-century myth.

But what of the historical Pope upon whom our author has based his narrative? The latest writers who have been bold enough to enter the arena have given us to understand that she is a fiction. This view, needless to say, is not shared by Royidis who has devoted several pamphlets to the subject. Did Pope Joan exist in truth? The whole position is admirably summed up by Platina, and by the fact that he felt bound to include her in his Lives of the Popes. Nobody can claim that the evidence of her existence is more than circumstantial; yet if so serious an historian as Platina—himself a secretary to a reigning Pope, and a librarian to the Vatican—felt bound to include Pope Joan in the canon of the Popes, we must conclude that the force of tradition, from many sources and for many years, must have dictated this distasteful choice. Here is her biography, as given in Platina:

'POPE JOHN VIII: John, of English extraction, was born at Mentz and is said to have arrived at Popedom by evil art; for disguising herself like a man, whereas she was a woman, she went when young with her paramour, a learned man, to Athens, and made such progress in learning under the professors there, that, coming to Rome, she met with few that could equal, much less go beyond her, even in the knowledge of the scriptures; and by her learned and ingenious readings and disputations, she acquired so great respect and authority that upon the death of Leo (as Martin says) by common consent she was chosen Pope in his room. As she was going to the Lateran Church between the Colossean Theatre (so called from Nero's Colossus) and St Clement's her travail came upon her, and she died upon the place, having sat two years, one month, and four days, and was buried there without any pomp. This story is vulgarly told, but by very uncertain and obscure authors, and therefore I have related it barely and in short, lest I should seem obstinate and pertinacious if I had admitted what is so generally talked; I had better mistake with the rest of the world; though it be certain, that what I have related may be thought not altogether incredible.'

So much for the historical position of the she-Pope whose life has been the subject of theological controversy from the Middle Ages until today. There have been numerous pamphlets written about her but nothing of the interest and freshness of this slight novel; but perhaps I should signal a lost Elizabethan play which figures on the long checklists of Henslowe's Diary. The name of the author is not given and the text has not survived, but it is amusing to find the she-Pope figuring on a list which includes names like Marlowe and Shakespeare; the subject matter might well have tempted the former but . . . speculation is useless unless the play itself should one day turn up to challenge comparison with Royidis' small work. It is doubtful whether any positive evidence for or against her existence will ever be unearthed, but so long as the myth can give us fiction as sparkling as *Papissa Joanna* we should not grumble too much. The historian may cry, 'Pope John VIII is dead', but he will hardly forbear to add—under his breath perhaps—'Long Live Joanna'.

And now having performed the formal act of introduction to the double entity—Pope Joan as history, and Pope Joan as literature—it only remains for me to commend her to the 'clement' reader whom Royidis so often invoked as he wrote—and whom, he said, she had never yet encountered in her native Greece.

I do not know whether it is good literary form to dedicate other men's books to one's own friends: but I have taken the liberty of inscribing this edition of *Pope Joan* to that giant of modern Greek scholarship and good humour Mr George Katsimbalis, who occupies in modern Athenian literary circles the position of a Dr Johnson. I think there is not a student or translator but owes him a debt for his work in the various fields of modern Greek literature; and I can think of no more suitable recipient for a dedication on the title page of the present book. Royidis would have agreed, had he been living. Indeed it was he, Katsimbalis, who first brought the book to my notice in 1939, in the course of one of those long growling walks about the purlieus of Athens—walks made so vivid by the discursive conversation of one of the world's best talkers. We stopped before a bookshop window in which a copy of *Pope Joan* lay, cockling slowly in the sunlight. 'Now there's a good book,' growled Katsimbalis, jabbing the window-pane with his huge stick, and rolling from one leg to the other. 'It is a typical scamp of a book, a Greek book, full of good fun, bad taste, and laughter and irreverence.'

I cannot see how a reader who values any of these qualities in his writers could fail to agree.

LAWRENCE DURRELL

Part One

'Il y a bien de la différence entre rire de la religion, et rire de ceux qui la profanent par leurs opinions extravagantes.'

PASCAL *Lettre XIe Provinciale*

THE EPIC POET usually begins in the middle of everything. Novelists, too, are rather apt to do the same thing – and roughly a tenth of their work might be classified as prose poetry. Thus the hero, while he happens to be stretched out in a cave or a palace, on a couch or on a bed of down, is in the habit of recapitulating all that has gone before for the benefit of his beloved. 'Having offered love sufficient sacrifice' . . . etc. You know the tag.

Such is the usual method, a form much urged on us by the critic. But I, while being a friend of the rule, much prefer the methods of the saga-writer or public prosecutor who, when he comes to describe the hero or a rogue, catches him in the cradle, as it were, and by following him chronologically leads him up to immortality or the gallows. Therefore in order to begin I must begin at the beginning – and anyone who prefers a classical disorder can read the last pages of this book first and the first last; thus transforming it at will from a plain unvarnished tale to an epic.

No less a personage than the great Byron himself had patience enough to listen to the chaffering of the old women of Seville in order to discover whether the mother of his hero said the Lord's Prayer in Latin, whether she knew Hebrew, and whether or no she wore a linen skirt and stockings. I would also like to tell my reader – if not all these details at least the name of my heroine's ancestors: but despite my rummagings among the stories of every medieval Herodotus I can only discover that her father had names as many and various as ever Zeus got from the poets or the Devil from the Hindus.

After spending several years over my manuscripts in the hope of discovering whether Joanna's family line descended through the Willibalds or the Willifrids, I have been reluctantly forced to doubt the adequacy of public rewards for such labours. So, taking my cue from the wise men of the day, who seem afraid to take time off in reading lest they should write less and thus deprive posterity of something valuable, I take up the thread of my narrative – or rather, I begin it.

Now the unknown father of our heroine was an English monk, though from which shire he came I have not been able to determine, as in those days Britain had not yet been divided into shires for the convenience of the tax-collector. His ancestors were those Greek apostles who had been among the first to plant the Cross in the green fields of Ireland. He was a pupil of John Scotus Erigena,[1] the first to devise a method for the wholesale manufacture of ancient manuscripts by which he hoodwinked the learned men of his time, just as Simonides[2] did the Berliners of his time. These facts alone has history left us about the father of Joanna.

As for her mother, her name was Judith. She was blonde and a goose-girl to a Baron. This noble Saxon, coming down one day to select the fattest among the geese for a feast he was to give, found his inclinations warm no less keenly towards the goose-girl than towards her geese: and translated her in one moment from the poultry yard to the bedroom. Bored with her after a while, he gave her to his cup-bearer, who gave her to the cook, who in his turn bestowed her upon the pot-boy. This last, being of a signal devoutness, exchanged her with a monk for the holy tooth of Saint Gutlhac[3] who, according to the legend, lived and died in great purity in some Mercian ditch. So it was that Judith fell from the couch of her master to the breast of a monk; as in England today the top-hat has fallen from the head of the diplomat to that of the beggar. For in that admirably governed country, while a fair number die from want, and while others outrage modesty for want of a shirt, yet all, parliamentarians and grave-diggers, earls and beggars, alike, wear the top-hat as a symbol of their constitutional equality.

The marriage was a happy one. During the day the monk trotted from castle to castle selling prayers and holy chaplets; in the evening he would return to his cell, his hands beslobbered with the kisses of the faithful, and his sack filled with bread, pasties, cakes and nuts. Potatoes were as yet unknown to England. They were introduced later together with a constitution for the governance of that free people; for when rational equality reigned servants found they could no longer eat even the crumbs from their masters' tables.

Judith, when she heard her husband's singing in the valley below, would set up the table – that is to say she set out on some rough boards their common platter, the iron fork, the cup of buffalo-horn, and she stacked the hearth with dry kindling to light their meal. Napkins, bottles and candles were then known only to bishops. After their evening meal the newly-weds spread out their sheepskins on a pile of dry leaves, lay down and drew over them a heavy wolfskin. The more harsh the north wind, the more thick the winter snow, the more closely they hugged each other, this contented pair: thus proving that St. Anthony was under a misapprehension about cold weather freezing love no less than the Greeks who called winter a woman-hater.

So they passed many happy days, the parents of Joanna 'In the midst of tender caresses': until one morning as the monk shook the sleep out of his eyes and some of his wife's blonde hairs out of his beard, two Saxon archers appeared at the door of the cabin.

They stood upon the threshold half-naked and bare of foot, carrying long shields and quivers full of arrows at their backs, and as they stood there they bawled out that in the name of Heptarch Egbert they ordered the householder to follow them without delay, and bring with him sufficient provision for a long journey. The scared monk slung a wallet over his arm and, taking his wife by the hand and his staff in the other, followed the frowning men, firmly clutching a prayer book in his armpit. They travelled for three days and nights through moors and valleys and over bare mountains, meeting on the road with other groups of holy men under the supervision of archers. On the fourth day they arrived at the little sea-port of Garyon.[4]

17

Crowds were gathered at the quay to which they were led by the guards. On a grassy mound stood the good Bishop of Eboracum,[5] Volscius by name. He was engaged in blessing all the faithful in a big Saxon ship that was quivering in the harbour as if eager to untie its square sails and turn them to the distant winds of the wide world. When the conscripts to the number of sixty, gathered from the four corners of England, stood there before him, Volscius gathered each in turn to his bosom and gave each a dole of two denars.

'Go,' he said, 'and preach to all the nations.' And from the arms of the bishop each of the missionaries was firmly led to the deck of a cavernous ship. They soon found themselves upon the turbid waves of the German Sea hardly knowing upon what foreign shores they were to find crowns of golden martyrdom or the precincts of some greasy monastery.

Now as they sail on under the divine protection of the Cross, I would like to pause in order to inform the reader what exactly was in the mind of the good bishop Volscius that he should commend to the mercy of the waves so many of the ornaments of the English Church. In order to do this, however, we must bid farewell to the Britons and enter the land of the Franks.

The great Charles, after capering all over Europe, reaping heads and laurels alike with his long sword, after strangling, blinding or mutilating three-quarters of the Saxon world and thus obtaining the respectful submission of the rest, was taking a short rest at last with all his trophies round him. He was at Aix-la-Chapelle, a city as justly famed for its holy relics as for its needles. All was going well with his vast Empire. The wise Alcuin[6] was busy bathing his dirty subjects in the sacramental waters of baptism, cutting off their red beards and long nails, and opening to a few the treasuries of an inexhaustible wisdom; he was sweetening the lips of others with the honey of the Word, or instructing them in grammatical roots, or teaching them that the same goosequill which speeds an arrow can also serve for writing. The happy Emperor spent his days with little to do except count the eggs his chickens laid, play with his daughters and his elephant – a gift from the Calif Aroun – and to track down guilty murderers and bandits on whom he imposed a small fine: while those of his subjects who ate meat on Fridays or were caught spitting after Communion were hanged from the branches of trees.

Now while the pious Charles,[7] who knew his classics though he did not know how to write, was repeating to himself each day *Deus nobis haec otia fecit*, the Saxons once more raised their daring if unbarbered heads, and plunging their arms in the blood (not of bulls this time but of human victims), swore by Thor, Wotan and Erminsul[8] that they would shake off the Charlish yoke or let the Elbe and the Weser run with their blood. As usual, however, the Emperor came, saw and immediately conquered. He carried in his hand that same lance which, the Evangelists state, had been used by a Roman soldier to pierce the side of the Saviour, and which had later been placed beside Charles's bed while he was asleep by the Archangel Michael: as a reward, so it is said, for his having refrained from cooked meat during Lent and from uncooked by sleeping alone. Afraid that he might be compelled by the Saxons to divert his interest from holy affairs, the Emperor Charles decided that extermination would be best for them or, failing that, baptism whether they liked it or not.

No other missionary succeeded in so short a time in christianising so many unbelievers. The eloquence of the Gallic conqueror was invincible. 'Believe or die,' he told the Saxon prisoner, in whose eyes the glitter of the executioner's sword shone with the light of persuasive argument. The mob jammed the fonts as geese do ditches after rain.

But inasmuch as it is necessary, however potent the faith, for the Christian to have some idea of what he believes, as it is today in Tahiti and Malabar, it became clear that some sort of a catechism ought to be instituted. This was left in the hands of Charles's corporals who instructed the new recruits by arranging them in rows of ten and hitting them mercilessly whenever they halted and found the words 'I believe' too difficult to pronounce. In this way

Jesus was receiving justice from those other idols that plagued his first followers, when they were burned alive under Nero or blinded under Diocletian. Hence also the French proverb which says: *La vengeance est le plaisir des dieux.*

While the war was actually being fought the soldiers performed the duties of the priests but when things grew calm once more and the theological knowledge of the missionaries was exhausted, everyone – and most of all the Emperor – felt that there was a growing need for more serious catechisers. Unhappily among the Franks the monks were rather more skilful at mulling wine than in absorbing religious dogmas; they baptised children in the name of the Father, Daughter and Holy Ghost, insisted that God's mother was conceived by the ear, breakfasted before taking communion, and forced the deacon to drink the water in which they washed their hands before Mass. In the hands of such instructors Charles felt it was impossible to trust even this Saxon rabble; in a short time, he felt, another expedition might become necessary to overthrow new idols to Bacchus and Morpheus. While hesitating about a course of suitable action he consulted Alcuin, in whose oracular pronouncements the Franks of those days took refuge very much as the Greeks did in the utterances of Pythia. Alcuin was British and Britain had at that time as complete a monopoly in theologians as she has today in locomotives. So it was that a ship was sent there to gather a group of missionaries for the initiation of the Saxons into the mysteries of the true faith.

The Christian ark which carried Joanna's father and his wife as passengers beat about for eight days before it passed the mouth of the Rhine and arrived, on the ninth, in the harbour of Nimegue where these soul-seekers touched German soil for the first time. From this point some travelled on asses, some in boats, some on foot, to the springs of Lippi, arriving at last both tired and hungry at Paderborn where Charles was then encamped, encircled by shields and crosses dug into the ground. The victorious Charles immediately parcelled Saxonia out among the monks, commending each one to have every house in his parish decorated by a cross. Joanna's father was ordered south to Erisburg where he was to pull down the idol of Ermensul round which the revolutionaries were wont to gather, as today they do in Haftia Square of Athens, and where they had begun to offer human sacrifices again, and to launch conspiracies almost daily. The miserable monk, loading his donkey with his wife and four loaves of black Saxon bread, started on his journey, tugging at the bridle of the animal, feeling the tears sting his eyes when he remembered the rude comforts of his native hut.

For eight years the father of Joanna now wandered under the trees of Westphalia preaching, baptising, hearing confessions, and burying. He became a far greater sufferer than the Apostle Paul for he was beaten innumerable times, was ten times stoned, was thrown into the Rhine on five occasions and twice into the Albis, was four times burned and thrice hanged, and yet despite all this still lived on with the help of Our Lady. For those sceptics who might doubt the truth of this account, I would add that reference may be made to the great Legendary of that day, from which it will be learned how the blond Virgin propped up the feet of the faithful when they were hanged, extinguished flames on a lighted pyre with a fan made of angel's wings, and untied her blue girdle which she held out to the drowning much as Ino did when she offered Ulysses her veil.

None of these sufferings, however, qualified the zeal or altered the mind of the untiring missionary though his body gradually became almost unrecognisable, for the Frisians had put out his right eye, the Longobards had lopped off his ears, the Thuringians his nose: while the untamed inhabitants of the Erlking forests, wishing to exterminate the future offspring of the missionary, first sacrificed his two children on the altars of Teuton and then, with the same inhuman knife, amputated his . . . every hope of paternity.

Judith, who remained still faithful to him, even after his latest mutilation, tried in every way to relieve the burden of his sorrow. Often when he woke at night and desired her, vainly blinking at her with his one eye and mourning his lost children no less than his extinguished pleasures, she kissed him tenderly, saying: 'Every day I light a candle at the altar of St. Paternus. Perhaps this patron of fertility will answer us and devise some way of having more children.' Alas! for the wish of the good Judith, for it was fulfilled quite soon; not by a miracle of St. Paternus[9] so much as by two of the earl's archers from the house of Erfurt. These two mischief-makers encountered her on the banks of the Fulda where she was spreading out the wet tunic of her husband on a bush – while he having nothing else to wear, crouched under cover of the bushes like Ulysses, waiting for the article to dry. The archers spread her, too, out on the grass and reminded her rather forcibly of the destiny of woman on this earth. When they had satisfied themselves and left, the unfortunate monk emerged from his hiding-pace and put his tunic on wet as it was, cursing the Saxons who had, as it were, given him a pair of horns to add to the halo of martyrdom which encircled his bald head.

Nine months after this, in the year 818, Judith was delivered in Ingelheim (or, as some say, in Mayence) of that future inheritor of the keys of heaven, Joanna. As she was born among the rigours of their wandering life, her father – or rather the husband of her mother – baptised her in the icy stream of Meinengen, where the inhabitants often plunged their swords to temper the blades.

The biographer of every Hero is in the habit of ornamenting the cradle of his subject, after the ancient manner, with stupendous augurs, in this way announcing the dawn of future faculties and virtues. So it is that we hear of Hercules strangling dragons in his infancy and Criezoti[10] the bear: while bees are supposed to have settled on the lips of Pindar, and Pascal to have invented geometry at the age of ten. Now just as the hero of Byron while attending mass in the arms of a nurse turned his eyes away from the dried-up saints to fix them with the greater emotion upon the Magdalene, so our heroine, who was to carve a career in the ecclesiastical world, showed her tendency immediately by refusing the teat if it were offered to her on a Wednesday or a Friday: and if ever it should be offered her during the Fast she averted her eyes in horror. Her first toys were crosses, relics and rosaries. She knew the Lord's Prayer in English, Greek and Latin before she cut her teeth; and before her milk teeth were out she was assisting her father in his missionary work by catechising Saxon girls of her own age. Though she was only eight when her mother Judith died she nevertheless delivered the funeral oration herself, climbing upon the shoulders of a gravedigger the better to do so.

Now while Joanna was growing daily in beauty and wisdom, her father, racked by pain and cast down by the loss of his wife, felt himself daily sinking. In vain did he appeal to St. Geno to steady his trembling shanks: in vain light candles to St. Lucia asking her to strengthen his eyesight so that he might yet read the psalter; in vain did he ask St. Fortio to strengthen his voice. His hands shook so that one day when offering the Body of Our Saviour to the beautiful Gisla, Abbess of the monastery of Bitterfield, he dropped it into the white bosom which this slave of Christ left bare by special permission of Pope Sergius. The scandal was tremendous. The recipient of communion turned scarlet, the nuns covered their faces with their hands, and the local priests cried aloud: 'Sacrilege.' And faithful to the echo the lonely virgins took up the cry as they tore at the wretched old man like Bacchae, wrenching off his ritual garments and propelling him out of the monastery.

For fifteen days the unfortunate missionary wandered with Joanna, among the inhospitable forests between Frankfort and Mogontia, spending the nights asleep under trees, and dining on acorns with the pigs of Vestulia. But this diet, while it fattened these brothers of St. Anthony, made the poor monk and his daughter in a short space of time as lean as the seven ears of corn in the dream of Pharaoh. In vain did the monk try to repeat the miracle of his compatriot, St. Patrick, who purely by his prayers turned wild boars of the Irish fells into fat hams; equally futile was his pleading with the eagles which flew overhead to fetch him food as they did for St. Stephen. Joanna, now and then, as she raised her dewy eyes to her father was constrained to cry: 'I'm hungry, dad.' At first the loving father would lift his withered arms to heaven and reply like Medea: 'I shall open my veins and feed you with my own blood.' But hunger gradually dried both his throat and his heartstrings, and to the wail of his daughter he answered dryly: 'Keep going.'[11]

The motion of a lamp led Galileo's mind around to the construction of the timepiece; and our hungry monk, by the same token, learned a method of keeping alive by his observations of a white bear. Observing one of these hairy polar maidens dancing at a local festival while her master collected money from the spectators, he decided to make use of the precocity and wisdom of Joanna, and profit from it as the trainer did from the bear, in order to gain his daily bread and small beer from it. How rightly, then, did Erasmus observe somewhere that a sensible man can learn a number of useful things from a bear. So the old monk began to prepare his daughter for her new profession by stuffing into her ten-year-old head much of the rubbish that wise men of the day termed Dogmatism, Daimonology, Scholasticism – or whatever else they called it in their parchments from which they had carefully scraped off every trace of the Homeric hymns or Juvenal's epigrams. When he thought her sufficiently primed in her subject to be able to undertake the struggle they started to make a tour of the castles and monasteries in the thickly wooded vale of Vestula.

As they entered a castle the old monk would kneel very reverently at the feet of the master, bless the mistress, extend his arms or his belt to be kissed by the servants, and then, placing Joanna on a table, he would being their act.

'Tell me, daughter,' he would say, 'What is tongue?'

'Air's whip.'

'What is air?'

'The element of life.'

'What is life?'

'For the happy a pleasure, for the poor a torture, to all an expectation of death.'

'What is death?'

'Exile on unknown shores.'

'What are shores?'

'Boundaries of the sea.'

'What is the sea?'

'A home for fishes.'

'What are fishes?'

'Delicacies of the table.'

'What is a delicacy?'

'The achievement of a great cook.'

After a sufficiency of this kind of question and answer which-displayed a general knowledge extending from theology to cooking, the old monk would invite the confessor of the castle to examine the girl in any branch of human knowledge that he liked; while Joanna, casting her hook into the ocean of her memory, always drew up the correct answer, often supporting it with a verse from the scriptures or a text from Boniface. After the inquisition she would jump softly from the table, and making a tray of her apron by gathering in its corners, she would pass before each in turn and ask with a sweet smile for their indulgence. Some tossed her copper coins, some silver, while some gave her eggs or apples, and those who had nothing, a kiss on the blond forehead of the young preacher.

They lived like this for five years and more, eating every day – and often twice a day – and passing many a night under the oaken panels of some noble's castle, or again under the thatched roof of a forester or trapper. The passing of the years and the memory of his former misfortunes had somewhat dimished the zeal of the old missionary, so that now he made no attempt to catechise the unwilling or to baptise without full consent any but the dead which he found on the banks of the Albis and the Rhine after a great battle. And even these he abruptly stopped baptising when he recalled that, according to the belief of the day, baptism of the dead would open to them the golden gates of heaven.

After years of this vagabondage the old man travelled himself one day to those unknown shores from which there is no return. Death took him while he was in the cell of the good hermit Arculfo who lived on the banks of the Mein, singing the praises of the saints and weaving wicker baskets for the fishermen. Joanna, having reverently shut the eye of her father, buried him with the hermit's help under a willow tree at the mouth of the river, engraving upon the tree-trunk an epitaph which set forth the virtues of the departed. This done the poor girl cast herself upon the soil that hid the only protector she had known in this world and mixed her salt tears, as did the wife of Othello, with the waves that wetted her small feet. After offering this libation of piety to the paternal ashes she wiped away those useless tears. Grief that we feel for the loss of someone very near to us resembles the extraction of a tooth – the pain is sharp but instantaneous. It is only the living who can cause us permanent pain. Who has ever poured out at the grave of his loved one, half, a hundredth, even a thousandth part of the tears he shed daily for her cruelty in life?

When Joanna stopped her tears she bent her head down to the water's surface to cool her burning eyes. For the first time she gazed with attention at her own reflection mirrored there and appraised the one creature time had left in the world for her to love. Let us lean over her shoulder and look upon the reflection in the racing mirror.

Face of a sixteen-year-old, rounder than an apple, blond hair of Magdalene but uncombed as Medea's, lips as red as a cardinal's biretta which promised inexhaustible pleasures, breasts plump and soft as partridges, still heaving with emotion. Such was Joanna when she caught a glimpse of herself in the water, and indeed it was thus that I myself saw her in an illuminated manuscript at Cologne. In some way that revelation eased the pain of our heroine who now stretched herself out upon the grass and propping her chin with her hand began to wonder how she could make use of so much beauty and wisdom; whether she should take the veil or find herself another protector like her father. After some time of drowsy reverie, teased by the burning heat and seduced by the chirping of the cicadas she fell asleep in the shade of a tree which protected her alike from the sun and from the gaze of the curious.

Now I have no idea whether Joanna had ever read Lucian, but when she closed her eyes she saw a vision not unlike that of the Samosatian. Two women appeared before her, coming out of the water. One of them had her breasts bare and wore flowers in her hair and smiled. The other in a black cassock with a cross at her breast had a look of great devotion. Both were very lovely, the beauty of one seeming to recall carnivals of laughter, the clink of glasses, and the drumming of dancers' feet; the dewy-eyed looks of the other spoke of the mysterious enjoyments of the abbeys, the noiseless banquets, the quiet kisses. As for the first, one would have longed to encircle her waist in some riotous dancing-place brimming with lighted candles, under the eyes of numberless spectators; as for the second, one would kneel before her in a silent cell under the faint light of the lamp hanging before the imagine of a saint.

As the two women approached Joanna, the former, running on ahead of her companion, addressed her, at the same time running her fingers lovingly through the blond locks of our heroine. 'I saw you,' she said, 'hesitating here between a wish for the world's pleasures and the silence of the monastery, and I ran at once to guide your inexperienced steps to the true pathway of happiness. I am St. Ida; there is not one good thing in this life that I have not tasted. I have enjoyed two husbands, three lovers, and seven children. I have emptied many a bottle of heart-warming wine, and passed many a sleepless night in pleasure. I have shown my shoulders to the world, have offered my hand to all lips, have let my waist be encircled by all who knew how to dance, and I am still worshipped and adored among the saints. All this pleasure I enjoyed while eating fish during Lent, throwing the crumbs of my table to the greedy mouths of priests, and giving them my old dresses to deck out the Virgin's statues. I can promise you the same future if you take my advice. You are poor, homeless and ragged; yet I too before becoming the wife of the Earl of Ecbert suffered from frozen fingers in winter; I too found that my only property was my own red lips, yet these brought me wealth, dignities and finally holiness. So have courage, my blond Joanna. For you are as lovely as the meadow-sweet is, wise as the book of Inamar, cunning as the fox of the Black Forest. With these things you can acquire everything delightful in life. Travel along the much-trodden road and let the foolish take the by-paths if they will. Find you a husband to give you his name and Spanish sandals: have lovers who will kneel down and kiss these sandals: have children to console you in your old age: and have, if you wish, the Cross in which you can take your final refuge whenever you tire of life or the living tire of you. This road and this only leads to happiness: the road I followed for thirty years among flowers, banquets, horses and songs, surrounded by husbands who loved me, by lovers who praised my loveliness, and by subjects who blessed my name. And when the end came I sank to rest on a purple bed, having tasted Communion from the hands of an archbishop, and supported by my children. Now I fearlessly wait for the Last Judgment, under the beautiful cold marble on which they engraved my virtues in letters of gold.'

Thus spoke Ida; and very much the same advice is whispered daily by experienced mothers in the ears of their daughters, promising salvation through the temporal and warning them against insipid novelists. Yet when she had unfolded the glittering chaplet of the world's pleasure before the eyes of Joanna her companion in the cassock came upon them and began to speak, her voice flowing as softly as the waters of Siloam. 'And I,' she began, 'am St. Lioba,[12] child; like you of Britain, cousin to the patron of that land, St. Boniface, I was a friend of the father you have buried under this earth.

'You have heard enough of the pleasures of the world from her.

Mixing together marriage, motherhood, passions and horseflesh, she concocted a gilded pill which she tossed to you as a good fisherman tosses his bait into the sea. But neither of the price nor of the defects of the treasure did our shrewd procuress speak. Ask her how often she shed tears because of the insults of her husband, how often for the infidelity of a lover, how often at the cradle of a sick child, how often before her mirror where instead of rosy cheeks and white arms she saw wrinkles and pallor look back at her?

'They were neither fanatics nor fools those early virgins who rejected the world and chose quietness in the shelter of some nunnery. For they knew that marriage was full of grievance when they first heard a woman in childbed or being beaten by her husband: when they saw their bellies puffed out and their breasts exuding milk: when they saw the wrinkles graven on their faces from sleepless nights and aches. It was the disgusting sight of the pregnant woman undressed or the woman giving suck that drove us into the nunneries. It was not a vision of angels and a taste for dry bread, as related by those old fools who wrote of the early saints. In the shade of the cell we found independence and rest, uninterrupted by the cries of children or the claims of a master, or any other care.

'Yet in order to keep the world from becoming deserted and the women from flocking to the nunneries and crowding us out we disseminated queer rumours about our way of life, such as that we spend whole nights kneeling on cold marble, watering staves till they bring forth flowers, sleeping in ashes, and flogging our bodies with the taws. For much the same sort of reason forgers used to circulate stories that the caves in which they made their counterfeit gold were haunted by ghosts and cruel vampires. Do not be afraid of the dry biscuit which St. Pachomius[13] nicknamed 'bread for nuns,' nor of the wretchedness of these garments for look what lies under them.'

As she said this, St. Lioba took off her dark cassock and emerged in a garment as fine as cobweb from Cos – contrived air, as the poets used to call it – and her body shone inside it like a strong wine in a crystal of Bohemian workmanship. Stooping to the ear of the sleeping Joanna she went on in an undertone. 'My rival promised you pleasures; but ask her if she ever enjoyed the pure sensations of the voluptuary in her lover's arms when her ear was alert, not for his sweet whispers but for every noise around her: turning pale and pushing him away whenever a door creaked or leaves rustled. Have you seen a cat climb on to a table to lap the master's milk? She looks sideways, cocking her sharp ears, her hair bristles with fear, her feet are ready to run away. So it is when these mistresses of the secular world taste what is forbidden.

'But we are surrounded neither by spies nor by cares but only by high walls and wooded groves. We pass the day conversing about pleasure as the ancient philosophers did before us. When vespers sound we retreat to our quiet cells where in silence and with emotion we prepare for pleasure as knights do for a duel. Dipping rough haircloth in tepid aromatics we rub the body until it begins to glow lambent as a rose, sensitive to every touch as a horse to the spur; after shaking out our long hair we cover the holy ikons and lie down, in winter near the glimmer of a cheering fire, in summer near an open window, listening to the song of a stray nightingale or the shaking of the leaves. As in the Song of Songs we give ourselves up to delicious dreams until at last, down the corridors, we hear the sandals of the coming one who will incarnate those dreams in flesh.

'The Oriental Greeks invented twin monasteries where the servants of the All Highest and the brides of Christ lived under the same roof divided only by a wall; but we perfected this invention of the Greeks by opening vents in these walls from whence, noiselessly and without danger, we could receive our brothers the Benedictines. We were the first to cultivate the sweet-smelling rue which would rid us of the cares of maternity, the strong clean smelling heather that insatiates the lips, and the stinging nettle from which our lovers draw new force as Antaeous from the earth.

30

'But do not imagine, Joanna, that we always confine our lives within four walls or limit them to such pleasures only. Sometimes satiety itself brings tedium; the journey of the sun seems far too slow as we watch it from behind the grilles of our cells, and the knights in coats of mail seem more desirable to us than our monks. Then it is that we feign some pilgrimage of piety to the grave of a saint and setting out we visit the people, enter their palaces and huts, visit their shows and baths, everywhere finding courteous hospitality and bowing heads.

'When I visited the court of the Emperor Charles we arrived on the night when they were celebrating his marriage with Hildegarde. Earls and their ladies, barons, and prelates were crowded in the chambers of the palace of Aquisgranum. The rhapsodists were chanting the exploits of the victorious bridegroom, the mimes and the morris dancers were making them all laugh with their queer antics, the dice were rolling and wine was going from hand to hand in silver-chased beakers. But when my black cassock appeared in the great doorways, when my name "Lioba, the abbess! Lioba the saint!" sounded in the saloons, all deserted their dice, their cups and their women to gather round and stare at me. Some kissed the buckle of my belt, some my footprints. The Emperor alone kissed my hands. My rude hairshirt covered the magnificence of the silk underneath, the diamonds I wore, my painted face and bare shoulders; while among the kneeling crowds my eyes picked out the eighteen-year-old Robert who raised dew-fresh eyelids and pressed his hands together as he searched for my face under the hood.

'When the festival ended I was led by the Emperor himself to the finest bedchamber of the palace, giving on to the park by a glass door. Awakening in the middle of the night I opened this door in order to lessen the odours of aloe and myrrh which had been sprinkled about the room to honour me; immediately opposite I saw Robert. He was sitting under an apple tree, elbows on his knees, and adolescent chin on hands, earnestly gazing at my window. When he saw me he rose, terrified and ready to fly, but with a motion of my head I invited him to enter my room. With a bound he was before me kneeling, but he neither touched me nor said a word; nor indeed did this poor boy dare to raise his eyes. When I put aside his long hair and searched with my lips for his forehead, thinking that he might take me for a ghost, he felt my dress, my hands, my untied hair to be sure that it was indeed I, St. Lioba, whom he held, half-naked and smiling in his arms. Which of the world's great courtesans proved worthy of such a worship? Which cast her lover into a stupor of passion more profound than I?

'Two full months I stayed in the palace of Charles; and when I was sated with feasting and hand-kissing and noise I said farewell to the hospitality of the palace. The Emperor himself held the bridle of my ass. The Empress and the princesses pleaded tearfully against my going. As for Robert, he tore his hair. Such a life I can promise you, Joanna; pure ecstasies instead of the gross pleasures of the people, independence instead of slavery, the abbess's discipline instead of the distaff, and Jesus instead of a mortal lover. You have heard Ida's advocacy of marriage, and mine of nunneries. Choose now between us, Joanna.'

The choice was not as hard as it may seem. In fact it could be made with both eyes shut. So it was without hesitation that our sleeping heroine held out her hands to the eloquent wearer of the cassock, while her companion, discountenanced and unable to refute her words, dissolved in a puff of smoke, as did those apparitions in female form that so disturbed the pious studies of St. Pachomius by placing a white bosom or red lips between his eyes and the breviary. St. Lioba kissed the new convert on the cheek and added joyfully: 'In order to be assured of your monastic vocation I did not tell you before what a thrice glorious future lies in store for you, and what a priceless reward it will bring. Semiramis became queen of the Assyrians, Morgana of the Britons, and Bathilde of the French. But you may see now what your fulfilled desire may be, Joanna. Look!'

Then a strange vision, a dream within a dream, dazzled the eyes of our heroine. She saw herself seated on such a high throne that her head, which wore a triple crown, almost touched the clouds; a white dove hovered near her and refreshed her with the air of its fluttering wing-beats. Crowds knelt at the foot of her throne; some were swinging silver censers from which the incense rose and condensed about her in sweet-smelling clouds; others scaled long ladders to reach her little feet and kiss them devoutly.

Did it ever, dear reader, happen to you to dream that you were being hanged from some high place, or that you were falling into some bottomless abyss? At the every instant when the rope tightens about your throat, or when your body is just about to be dashed to pieces, you wake up and find yourself in your warm bed, your nightcap on your head, your dog at your side. Nothing is more delicious than such awakening. You feel your limbs and exult to find them unhurt. You open your eyes wide and then the window so that the dream shall not visit you again. But if it ever happened that you dreamed a pleasant dream in which, shall we say, you discovered the philosopher's stone or a prudent wife, and that you woke up just as you hands were reaching out to grasp these chimerical treasures: why then, everything must have seemed stale and profitless to you. Repulsing the disagreeable reality you withdrew your head deeper under the covers and tried desperately to recapture those vanished ghosts. This was just the feeling Joanna had when she woke after the enchanting vision and found herself destitute, unprotected and alone near the freshly dug earth of her father's grave. The hospitable Arculfo came in a little while to offer food and consolation to the orphan but she, rejecting alike the good hermit's condolences and his gift of unsalted vegetables, asked him instead to direct her to the nearest convent.

'At Mosbach,' said the old man. 'There is one dedicated to St. Blittrude.' And he pointed with his trembling finger to the East.

Joanna thanked him and tightening her belt she followed the path he had shown her, hastening forward to the conquest of those joys which St. Lioba had promised her. And the pious hermit, watching the alacrity with which she departed, recorded in his diary that through his prayers the overshadowing trees of the hermitage had acquired, as it were, the peculiarity of inspiring an ungovernable impulse towards the monastic life in all those who had rested in their shadow.

Joanna, who in her anxiety to arrive, had not asked for an exact description of the route, continued along the open road like a hunted stag, but later on, becoming lost in a maze of thickets and rides she began to feel as Demeter did at the brink of the well, wondering if it were not better to stop and consider what best to do. Meanwhile night stretched moonless and gloomy over the woodland, and in the dark the sinister eyes of owls and wolves glimmered among the ferns and thickets. The unfortunate girl, alone in that fearful wilderness, sometimes remained immobile and silent by the trunk of an oak tree: and then, gaining strength from the awe-inspiring silence of the woods, flitted on like some nocturnal ghost among the trees. So she wandered on until, in the deepest part of the wood, she saw a dim light towards which she directed her steps, hoping to reach the hospitable shelter of a hermitage. But instead she found only a wooden statue of the Theotokos built into a hollow tree under which burned one of those miraculous lamps in which the oil never became exhausted – according to the accounts of some hagiographers of the day: others said, more credibly, that the oil was renewed each night by the angels. Joanna fell down before the image and prayed to the Virgin asking her protection and guidance so that she might find her way out of that woody labyrinth. Her prayers were heard. The threefold braying of donkeys answered the girl's prayers and in a short time the animals themselves appeared, bowed under the weight of a trio of corpulent monks; a fourth donkey followed them, dragging a one-wheeled cart on which lay two oblong boxes, piously covered with embroidered silver cloth. The three mounted men, Brother Raleig, Leguin and Regibald, had been friends of Joanna's father, and they were travelling to Mulinheim with the bodies of those martyred saints, Peter and Marcellinus.

Our heroine was allowed a seat on the cart which carried the

34

relics; and when the good fathers had heard Joanna out they began to tell her of their own journey to Rome where they had been sent by their Abbot, Eginhard, to buy holy relics. As they were unable to bargain they had gone under cover of darkness, led by an angel with a lamp, to the crypts of St. Tiburtius' church, and by its light they had opened the graves of Peter and Marcellinus and stolen their bones which they had succeeded in conveying to Germany after many vicissitudes and dangers.

At first the saints had been somewhat indignant at being so exhumed and having their rest disturbed; many a protesting moan and groan had been heard from the coffins, and drops of holy blood were seen every day falling from them. But now they had become more or less submissive in the face of destiny and had resumed some of their former habits like working miracles, curing the lame, the blind and the paralytic, banishing evil spirits, transforming beer into wine, ravens to doves, and pagans to Christians. These and many other things did the good fathers narrate to Joanna, praising the good work of their saints as male prostitutes once praised their Syrian goddess. But the honeyed promises of St. Lioba still rang in the ears of Joanna, and she gave little enough heed to her fellow travellers and their saintly legends, yawning several times in the course of their narrative, until at last she fell fast asleep, lying between St. Peter and Marcellinus. Fearing that the same thing may happen to you, my female reader, we would direct your attention to the next chapter for the continuation of our simple story.

Part Two

'Regrettez-vous le temps où nos vieilles romances
Ouvraient leurs ailes d'or vers un monde enchanté,
Où tous nos monuments et toutes nos croyances.
Portaient le manteau blanc de leur virginité?'

MUSSET ROLLA

HAS IT EVER happened to you, dear reader, that when you had passed a day reading a novel about the Middle Ages, such as the exploits of King Arthur or the loves of Launcelot and Guinevere, that you let the book fall as you began in your mind to compare the past age with the present, longing once more for those times when reverence, patriotism and unadulterated love still ruled the world? Those times when faithful hearts burned under steel breast-plates, when pious lips kissed the feet of the Crucified; when queens wove tunics for their husbands and virgins waited for years in the quiet rooms of their castles for their returning lovers; when the illustrious Roland withdrew from public life to a cave opposite the nunnery where his beloved was shut up and spent thirty years only looking at the light in her window? Frequently among such reveries I felt my blood warm and my eyes grow moist with emotion.

But when I left the rhapsodists to seek out the truth buried beneath the dust of centuries in the chronicles of contemporaries, in the laws of kings, the memoranda of Synods, the decrees of Popes: but when I say, in the place of Hersart I looked into Baronius and Muratori, when I beheld the Middle Ages stripped and naked before me: then I was forced to bemoan the fact, not that such days had passed, but that these golden fabulous epochs had never appeared in that world of blind faith and heroism.

We left Joanna travelling with two saints, three monks, and four asses. The route they took was tenebrous and winding – as involved as the prose style of the New School – so that both humans and animals grew weary after trudging for two hours. And when they caught sight of a red lantern shining on the summit of a neighbouring hill, they directed themselves eagerly towards that beacon of salvation as did the Magi towards the star which showed them the way to the Manger.

From the days of Tacitus until now gluttony and wine-bibbing have been the prevailing sins of the German race; but at least the hospitable inhabitants of ancient Germany became drunk in their own cottages, where they were always ready to offer supper and shelter to the weary traveller. But the monks of the Middle Ages, after St. Benedict[14] had replaced wine with beer on the tables of the cenobia, were compelled to resort to the taverns very much as the ancient Greeks went to the agora. In vain did the Synods and Pope Leo anathematise the sellers and drinkers of wine; in vain did hospitable hermits found roadside hermitages on the highways and in the woods, offering the wayfarer free hospitality – green vegetables for table fare and dry hay to sleep on. In bad weather travelling monks would sometimes enter these cells, but the minute the rain stopped they took themselves off again – to the nearest tavern.

Today the inns are established for the sake of the travellers but during the Middle Ages many a monk turned traveller for the sake of the inns. The three good fathers after stabling the donkeys, placing the holy relics on the innkeeper's bed, and their persons in front of the fireplace (there is no such thing as a summer night in that country), lifted their noses to smell the fragrance which was being wafted to them from the kitchens. A plump goose was turning on a spit over a glowing mound of coals; another was stewing in the good wine of Ingelheim. The sight of the spit and the song of the pot delighted the hearts of the good fathers who seated themselves without further fuss around a stone table and were beginning to sharpen their knives and their teeth in order to be prepared for their prey when suddenly an importunate memory darkened their gaiety like a cloud.

'Friday,' announced Raleig, pushing back his platter. 'Friday,' replied Leguin putting down his fork. 'Friday,' shouted Regibald, and clapped his large mouth shut, as they stared all three at the geese as Adam once stared at his lost Paradise. They began to bite their nails in despair. In those times men were, of course, both crapulous, gluttonous and impure. They were swindlers. But they had not yet sunk low enough to touch meat on a lenten day. The Paradise of those times, like Olympus for the ancients, was ruled over by the sacred patrons of drunkenness, while of course on earth the bishops permitted such indulgence, holding it to be according to the example of the Ecclesiastes and of holy Augustine himself. But whosoever did not observe Lent was either threatened with purgatory or else hanged out of hand from a high tree by the Emperor's bodyguard.

Joanna, knowing from experience what hunger is, was sorry for her hungry comrades. Clever as she undoubtedly was in casuistry, a science as yet unknown to Easterners, by which black bread can be proved to be white, the moon square rather than round, virtue to be vice, and so on, she had difficulty in attempting to devise a way by which they might eat and yet not be fallible. For some time, after pondering and scratching her head, she was silent. Then she suggested, 'Why not baptise the goose for a fish and then you may eat it without fear. So did my poor father when he was captured by the savages and forced, under pain of death, to devour a whole lamb on the evening of Easter Sunday. Besides, fishes and birds were created on the same day, so their flesh is related.'

The argument if not completely water-tight was at least gallantly attempted; and hunger, which can make the dryest bread seem tasty, has a knack of reinforcing the most precarious of arguments. It is true that brigands are often acquitted when they plead that their offence was committed when they had been without food for some time. The same sort of reasoning ought to apply, when you think of it, to those guilty of rape who can prove, according to Theocritos, 'an urgent need.'

Brother Raleig, thanking Joanna with a sound kiss on the cheek, took a cup of water and sprinkled the geese thrice repeating piously: '*In nomine Patris, et Filii et Spiritus Sancti, haec erit hodie nobis piscis.*' His companions responded with an 'Amen' and very shortly nothing remained of the recently baptised fishes except the bones. Having satisfied their hunger now the good brothers turned their thoughts to the quenching of their thirst – it being the habit of the day to eat until the point of satiety before asking for wine and salty condiments to cool and dry the tongue alternately: at the same time contesting round with round to see who could hold the most. At that time drunkenness was the cheapest of enjoyments, a gallon of wine costing about seven denarii; it flowed liberally not only in the taverns, but also in the streets and churches and even in the girls' schools, not in the least impeded by the decrees of the Popes and the Synods. According to the manners of the day each of our good fathers toasted first the name of one angel; then they started steadily to empty the horn-beakers again and again, not pledging absent friends or fatherlands as the normal custom is, but pledging the Virgin, St. Peter and all the inhabitants of Paradise. Such was the habit of those godly times which established inebriation as a condition pleasing to God.

Meanwhile the night drew on, the innkeeper went to sleep, the oil in the lamp not less than the wine in the cask was running out; only the good humour of the monks increased with every cup they drank. Their eyes glittered like the eyes of Charon, while half inarticulate sounds began to issue from their lips, blasphemies mingled with invocations to the Parthenos, hymns mingled with bacchic chants. Joanna, who knew that wine brought on profligacy and remembered that Solomon inveighed against debauchery while seated among three hundred wives and seven hundred concubines, retired into the darkest corner of the room. But even here she did not find rest for very long for the good fathers, having satisfied their hunger and thirst, felt it necessary to satisfy that sixth sense for which the physiologists have not yet found a name, though more modest chroniclers have called it a taste for raw meat. So, taking their cassocks between their teeth, as the expression is among monks, they rushed upon our very unhappy heroine.

Do not hasten to blush, my worthy female reader. The steel pen with which I write this true story is of English make and has come from the factory of Smith, which makes it as modest as those blond Englishwomen who, in order not to soil their spotless dresses, raise them above their knees, giving the passer-by a glimpse of their flat feet in double-soled sandals. No, there is no danger of hearing from me anything 'unbecoming to reveal before the virgin mind.'

Joanna, pursued by the three monks, ran about the room, leaping over tables and chairs, sometimes throwing a dish or a scriptural maxim at her pursuers. But her sacred eloquence and the table utensils alike broke in vain upon those drunkards as waves do upon rocks. When at last they stretched out their hands for her she noticed on the bed the relics of the saints and at once beat a retreat behind them. The monks withdrew at once from that sacred bulwark as wolves withdraw before the fires the shepherds light around their byres. But soon after, forgetting their respect for the sacred relics, they hurled themselves once more upon the bed where the wretched girl lay trembling like a lark in a hunter's net. The collision was so violent that it caused the bed to break and fall, and with it the boxes of the saints, whose martyred bones began rolling about the room. Joanna remembering that Samson once struck down a thousand Phillistines with a jawbone of a mere ass, prayed to the All Highest to strengthen her arm, and taking up one of the legs of St. Marcellinus, she started to batter at her lustful pursuers. But their bones seemed to be harder than those of the saints for in a short time the weapon broke and the strength of our heroine being exhausted after such a stubborn resistance she fell at last on the field of battle, submitting to her destiny. But at that time there were several saints miraculously working in order to save this virgin from danger.

At the moment when the Holy Brother Raleig, who as the eldest enjoyed preference of place, was bending over her, his vile and loathsome breath defiling the pale features of the girl – at that moment a monstrous transformation took place. An unearthly miracle made him withdraw in terror. Neither into a tree, like Daphne, was Joanna transformed: nor into a dove like St. Gertrude: nor into a worm-eaten and desiccated body like Bassina when she lay with Don Rupert: but from her virginal cheeks there sprang up all unexpectedly a long, thick beard – like one of those beards which loom on the faces in Byzantine ikons. This was the way the Virgin saved many a virgin in those times when she was molested by the rude monks. For she was as vigilant for their honour as a jealous mother-in-law for the honour of her son's wives according, that is, to St. Jerome.

Blessing the Virgin from her very heart for so timely an intervention, Joanna sprang up and wagged her long beard like the head of Medusa until the terrified monks ran from the room.

Then, going out to the stables, she untied one of the donkeys and mounted it, leaving behind her that disgusting haunt where she had been in danger of losing the only dowry she had to offer her heavenly bridegroom. Needless to say when the danger had passed the beard also vanished.

The shades of the night were lifting from the forest ways. Darkness had begun to disperse and make way for the daylight. After some hours of wandering our heroine found herself in the middle of a vale covered in bracken with a pure white sky overhead and a black donkey between her legs. Not knowing the road, Joanna had been letting the animal carry her wherever it wished, but now she discovered the bank of the Mein, and she took control once more to follow the winding of the river as Theseus once followed Ariadne's thread. At last she arrived, at the setting of the sun, at her journey's end.

The convent of Mosbach was built at the foot of a steep mountain; St. Blittrude had placed it there that the zeal of the nuns might not be cooled by the northerly winds. The evening prayer was ending at that moment and the nuns were coming out of church, two by two and hand in hand – resembling nothing so much as a rosary of black pearls. Seeing Joanna they gathered round her immediately, asking who she was, where she came from, and what she desired. When they heard that she sought a veil, a pair of sandals and a cell, they took her to the abbess who bethrothed our heroine to the Lord, freeing her from the ten-month probation because of her father's services to the Church.

St. Blittrude was immediately taken by the new nun and because of her erudition and knowledge appointed her to be librarian to the convent, which then owned sixty-seven volumes – a fabulous library for those times. Joanna, alone from morning to night in her cell, fell during the first few days into that enervation of soul which overtakes all newcomers to monasteries: similar to the malaise which afflicts those who travel by ship for the first time. Entering and leaving her cell, dusting her books, cleaning nails and hair, and counting the beads of her rosary, she felt somewhat inclined to censure the sun for travelling so slowly across the sky to its rest. Her comrades, envious of the influence she seemed to enjoy over the abbess, and afraid that she might spy upon their words or actions, kept apart from her with distrust. Frequently during the hour of recreation while the other young virgins expended their energies by wandering about the gardens in groups, talking hilariously to each other, pinching the elder women, showing each other notes from their lovers, comparing the size of their feet or the colour of their lips and hair, poor Joanna stood alone like an obelisk in the centre of the square, measuring the height of the trees and blaming St. Lioba that instead of pleasures she had found only tedium and boredom in the nunnery: very much after the fashion of those pioneers who blamed the newspapers because they found more stones than gold in California.

Despair and idleness are, I think, the chief motives for religious devotion. When we have nothing on earth to do or hope for we gaze at the sky. We kiss the holy ikons because we have nothing better to kiss. However Joanna, who had formerly employed her theological gift purely as a wage-earning device, now learned the scriptures and the books of the fathers by heart when she found herself alone in her suffocating little cell: as Madame Ristori

43

memorised the verses of Alfieri. So finding the present insipid she began to dwell upon the future life.

Monasteries have, throughout the ages, been realms which harbour rather specialised desires. The Egyptian monks watered staves until they yielded fruit; the women saints of Hungary devoured lice, while the Hesychasts lived for whole years in fixed contemplation of their navels from whence they expected the light of Truth to spring. And Joanna, surrendering herself to metaphysical studies, now spent whole days bowed over the writings of St. Augustine who has described, almost as an eye-witness might, the enjoyments of the blessed and the flames of Hell. Then pushing her fingers into her blond hair she would address to herself all those burning questions about our present and future life which the inhabitants of this vale of tears are wont to attack in desperation and which the priests and theologians answer with evasions and commonplaces, just as cabinet ministers do when they want to be rid of importunate place-hunters. Troubling dreams began to disturb the sleep of our heroine. They were no longer those of St. Lioba, promising her inexhaustible pleasures, but they were of devils waving fearful horns of fire, or angels holding large two-edged swords. At one moment she would hope for the joys of Paradise, at another be terrified by the claws of the devil. For one day at a time she would believe all the truths of Christianity, from the Gospels to the miracles of St. Martin – and then for three she felt uncertain of everything. Sometimes she would bow her head and humbly await the divine condemnation – at others she could have hurled boulders at the sky to shiver it into atoms. (The sky at that time was supposed to be of crystal.) In a word she was seized with that sort of monomania which preys upon all those who sincerely seek a solution to the mysteries of existence.

What are we? Where do we come from? What is to be our future state? Such were the questions, as insoluble to the human brain as wax in water, which Joanna tried to solve. In the meantime the hair of the poor girl was left uncombed and her teeth uncleaned; her eyes grew red from sleeplessness, her face pale, her nails black from neglect. According to the great Pascal such should indeed be the physical condition of the true Christian on this earth: to live continually between the fear of Hell and the hope of salvation, and with groans and cries to grope in the darkness for the road to Paradise. But that condition, aristocratic as it may be – even the prerogative of superior minds – that is not a condition I wish for you, my dear reader. I should rather consider it preferable to be merry, in the manner of those good Christians who sing hymns to the saints, eat cuttle-fish on Friday and wait, free from care, for the pleasures of Paradise. There will be some of course who wish to show their moral superiority by pitying those happy mortals, but for my part I envy their untroubled hearts and their rosy cheeks. If some Turk or some fire-worshipper of my acquaintance sought to become a Christian, I would counsel him to choose the Catholic Church above all others, for its ceremonies are sumptuous, its liturgy is brief, and its fasts are liberal. Its music delights the ear and its ikons the eye. As for his spiritual adviser, I would urge upon him not a savage one like Bossuet or Lacordaire (who descibes so vividly the tortures of Hades and its inhabitants) but rather a student of the honey-tongued Escobar, in order that he might be conducted to the heavenly mansions upon a carpet of satin. The All Highest, according to the holy Augustine and Lactantius, does not look askance at the choice of the more liberal paths provided they lead us towards Him, so what point is there in hunting for Paradise through thorns and thistles and boiled vegetables: in listening to nasal songs and kissing ugly images? But let us return to our subject, and blame these digressions on the fifty-seven newspapers of Athens and the four bells of the Russian church which are forever disturbing the continuity of my story.

The worst diseases such as plague, small-pox, and those others which were originated by Eros and his golden-haired mother, have at least one advantage: that we are subject to them only once. The metaphysical affliction of Joanna was in this category.

After three months of head-scratching as she sought the solution of the unfathomable riddle, she finally banged her books shut and opening her window sniffed the fragrance of spring. April was almost at an end, and everywhere nature was verdant, smiling and sweet-smelling, like a young lady dressed by a skilful maid-in-waiting. The scents of spring intoxicated the young nun who after three months of musing and metaphysics in the gloom of her cell smelled with growing hunger the scents of the grass in the meadows and the violets.

Between our hearts and the spring when we are twenty there exists, according to the poets and the doctors, a mysterious and inexplicable relation, like that of Socrates to Alcibiades. Whenever we look upon trees in leaf, soft grass or shady caves, we at once feel the want of a companion to season that Paradise. Joanna remembered the dreams and hopes she had nourished when she entered the nunnery to find in their stead ennui, old tomes, and disagreeable speculations. 'Lioba, Lioba, when will your promise be fulfilled?' she now cried out, shaking the bars of her prison in desperation. And not having a dog in her cell with her to beat, or any Chinese vases to break, she hid her face in her hands and started to weep. Now nothing is sweeter than tears when there is a ready hand to wipe them away for one, or a pair of lips eager to kiss away that rain of the heart, as the Hindus call it. But when one weeps alone, then tears are very true and bitter, like every truth in the world.

In a little while the noise of footsteps in the corridor outside distracted her attention from these painful speculations, and soon the door opened to admit the abbess who held by the hand a beardless young man, dressed in the robes of a Benedictine, and who remained staring at his own sandals with an air of solemn fixity. 'Joanna,' said the Mother Superior, presenting the young monk to our overcome heroine, 'the Abbot of Fulda, St. Rabanus the Black,[15] intends to send some preachers to Thuringia and has asked me for a copy of the Pauline epistles in gold on the best parchment. He hopes that the gold will dazzle the eyes of the infidels and inspire them with respect for the truth of the Gospels. This is Father Frumentius. He, like you, is distinguished for his devotion and calligraphy. You are to collaborate with him until the order of your Father Rabanus is carried out. Take gold-leaf ink for the task. You have pens. I shall send you food from my own table. Farewell, my children.'

Having said these words St. Blittrude left, closing the doors behind her as those peasants in Moldavia do whenever their master is visiting their wives. She was among those spotless women whose minds are incapable of harbouring evil. If she had seen a deacon kissing a virgin of the convent she would have imagined that he was conferring some sort of blessing on her. From childhood she had been scarred by small-pox and by consequence, having known only innocent kisses, she was incapable of believing that there would be any other kind. Besides all this, in that century the followers of St. Benedict, men and women, lived together anyhow in the monasteries. According to some writers their relations were of a spotless innocence, like those of St. Amoun who lived eighteen years with his wife who, when she died, was pronounced a virgin. But according to Muratori this cohabitation bred both scandals and offspring, though the latter were usually cast into the river of Fulda, thus saving the face of the monastery and feeding the fish.

The young pair when left alone like this, knowing how valuable time was, rolled up their sleeves and fell to work; that is, to the copying of the Pauline epistles. For fifteen days the young monk came to the cell of Joanna where he collaborated with her until nightfall. But that young eighteen-year-old, having read neither the Gospels nor St. Augustine's confessions nor St. Basil on virginity, nor any other holy book, was as spotless as the driven snow upon which St. Francis rolled to appease the temptations of the flesh. So while the copying of the Pauline epistles proceeded rapidly his relations with Joanna remained at a standstill.

Whenever the hand of our heroine touched his, whenever their hair interweaved as they bent low over the text, he felt his heart throb like the bell of a fortress in danger, but he was unable to say whether it was throbbing on his right side or his left. Now Joanna had made a point of reading Origen, Chrysostom, and the scholiasts who dealt with self-denial. She knew everything there was to know in theory. She could even discuss these subjects and use the technical phraseology known only to doctors, theologians and hetaerae. But this was the first time that she found herself alone with a man. Her confusion about what was to be done increased daily and she became as puzzled as English travellers when they find themselves in an unfamiliar place whose location they have so earnestly studied on the map.

The situation of the two young people became every day more wearisome, for neither did Frumentius know what to ask nor Joanna what first to offer. Meanwhile the copying neared its end. Only the Epistle to the Hebrews remained before the bitter and inevitable separation which must come upon them. Joanna, like another Penelope, took to scraping off at night what they had written during the day. Her companion understood the trick, fully foresaw her intentions. He blushed and emitted sighs capable of moving the sails of a windmill. But he limited himself to such expressions and the day passed like the rest, full of futile desires and disappointed hopes. But neither you, dear reader, nor I, have many days to lose. What is more, in writing a true story, I cannot imitate those poets and authors who heap up tremblings, tears, blushes, and other platonic provender, yoking their mellifluous lines by twos as husbandmen do oxen to the plough, and smoothing off their periods as round as the paps of Aphrodite. So abandoning these devices of Plato, Ovid, Petrarch and their mawkish followers I shall continue to describe the truth, naked and uncombed, just as it came up out of the well.

The lovers had just finished the copying of the last epistle when the sun, which Galileo had not yet condemned to immobility, was going through its diurnal rotation. It was the hour when the cows returned to the stable and when all good Christians kissed the image of the Virgin with an 'Ave Maria.' The bell had summoned the nuns to evening prayer and there was silence in the corridors of the convent. Joanna, sitting near the window, was busy skimming through a volume of the Scriptures while Frumentius stared ecstatically at his companion as the setting sun, shining through the stained glass window, threw a radiant circle about her head – like a saint's halo by a Russian painter. Our heroine, however, who was then seventeen, by no means resembled those pallid and angel-faced virgins whom one would not dare to touch for fear that they would open a pair of invisible wings; nor could she fairly be compared to a rosebud; but rather, let us say, to that plant of sunny Palestine which offers both fragrance and fruit to the weary traveller from the same branch. The shade of the cloisters and the convent's good table had strengthened the body and made more supple the skin of the beautiful Joanna; her hair, only once trimmed, rippled more thickly than ever over her shoulders. It is true that all these were, from a certain point of view, uncombed, untended, and neglected, but according to the poet gold needs no gilding, roses no extra scent, nor lilies a rosy hue; well neither for that matter does a girl of seventeen, I think, need curls and perfumes.

Frumentius continued to be silent and Joanna went on turning the leaves of her book, sometimes muttering between clenched teeth, sometimes reading a verse aloud. But after a while she ceased to skim and in a low pleasing voice, like that of a young Hindu charming a poisonous snake, she began to read aloud.

'The Song of Songs, which is Solomon's. Let him kiss me with the kisses of his mouth: for thy love is better than wine.

Because of the savour of thy good ointments thy name is as ointments poured forth, therefore do the virgins love thee. . . .

Stay me with flagons, comfort me with apples, for I am sick of love. . . .'

Frumentius hearing all this, and not realising that all these apples, breasts and kisses were prophetic allegories picturing the future love of the Saviour for His Church, felt like a second Job, his skin and hair set on fire with desire. With every verse of that heavenly incantation he took a step towards the reader; and when she came to the last verse he was there kneeling before her. Joanna then raised her head from the book and the eyes of the two lovers met. When one finds oneself at the brink of a precipice (and such was, I think, the position of our heroine) it is necessary, they tell one, to shut the eyes or one will get dizzy and fall. But Joanna kept her eyes open though she did not fall. Only the book fell from her hands.

Quel giorno più non vi leggero avanti.

The Prussian deputy at the peace conference which followed the Crimea requested an eagle's feather with which to add his name and titles to the treaty. I, however, wish I had a feather from the wings of Eros with which to describe the daily happiness of this young couple. Solitude, quietness, abundance, spring weather – none of these elements was missing to complete their happiness.

Joanna who had been excused matins because of the copying, not to mention the other studies, the prayers and monastic drudgeries in force there, was able to spend the whole day, from dawn to dusk with her companion. But though it was now June the days seemed far too short to these young people with insatiable lips and hearts. Often at the hour of vespers when the bells sounded forlornly from the steeple as they sat together at the open window they all but cried 'Stand still' to the sun as Joshua once did; but he was well on his way towards the antipodes and the two lovers would have to separate and wait for the following day.

They spent ten more days together in that narrow cell, writing, talking and kissing, and had no other complaint against the weather save that time passed too quickly. But at last came the ill-omened day of separation. The copies of St. Paul had long ago been finished and the Abbot sent a mule, with a verbal order to Frumentius to return to the fold once more. The unhappy young man, cursing his vows, his superiors and the whole gamut of saints, went to bid farewell to his companion. In his hand he held his pilgrim's staff. He could not restrain his tears. Joanna did not cry for some of her comrades were present; and women anyway only weep when and where it seems fit to do so – even the most impulsive of them. A splendid illustration of this may be seen among those easily moved Englishwomen who, when they go to hear Ristori, mark the proper places in Myrrha and Medea where tears may be shed.

But as soon as Joanna was alone once more she felt that sinking feeling in the pit of the stomach which always afflicts us after we have eaten too much, lost a mother or a lover, or even a fortune – at any rate something too difficult to replace from one day to the next. According to that much-admired old writer Plutarch women never even feel the shadow of true love. Certainly I think that for them it is a transitory illness, for only cold reason can be content with monotony and solitude. The women of the world passing from the arms of one man to another every night (I mean at the ball) have little enough time for sighs, nor indeed for much besides their fans; in this they are apt to resemble the donkey who remained hungry amidst four heaps of trefoil because it could not make up its mind which to choose. Probably I am mistaken about it, but at any rate all the amorous souls I have encountered have been girls locked up and guarded like the apples of the Hesperides by jealous parents, or ageing mistresses numbering more years than admirers.

The sadness of Joanna, once more alone between those four walls which had heard so many sighs and vows, heard so many kisses given and returned, became more desperate every day. St. Augustine when he grew despondent rolled in filth as in some delectable bath; St. Genevieve[16] shed tears so fast that she was forced to change her blouse; St. Francis hugged snow-covered statues; St. Libania tore her flesh with an iron comb, while St. Luitberga swallowed needles. But our heroine, wisest of all, lay quietly in the corner of her cell as with a fan of pigeon's feathers (the only sort allowed in monasteries) she tried to drive away the flies and her tormenting thoughts. The languorous heat of June made her affliction more difficult to bear and the days seemed as long as those of an ageing uncle to his heirs. Sometimes in paroxysms of desperation, and in an attempt to expel the importunate ghosts that haunted her, she took refuge in the holy precepts of the Book of Saints, whipping herself with her cassock-cord, saturating the sheets of her bed with icy water, or trying to solace her grief with wine, according to the counsel of Ecclesiastes. Yet all these wonder-working nostrums – and even that *agnus castus*, the odour of which, say the hagiographers, was strong enough to repulse temptation – availed her nothing against the bitterness of separation.

Time, they say, heals every wound; but not, I think, love or hunger. On the contrary, the longer anyone remains continent or fasting the more his appetite grows until he is ready to devour his own boots, like Napoleon's soldiers in Russia, or make love to his she-goats like the shepherds of the Pyrenees. It was while she was in this frame of mind that one evening, as she sat by the fish-pond despondently dividing her dinner among the carp, she observed the monastery gardener approaching her with a mysterious air, looking carefully about him as he did so. He delivered to her a letter written with purple ink on the thinnest skin of a new-born lamb. Opening it Joanna found (amidst flower-devices, pierced hearts, kissing doves, burning candles and other passionate symbols with which the lovers of that age ornamented their letters) the following message:

Frumentius to his Sister Joanna rejoicing in the All Highest
As the hart panteth after the water-brooks so panteth my soul after thee, my sister. – Psalms.

And let them make haste and take up a wailing for us that our eyes may run down with tears, and our eyelids gush out with waters. – Jeremiah.

The hungry dream of bread but I saw thee asleep, Joanna, yet waking found thee not. – Isaiah.

Going up then to my black ass I approached thy holy taber-
nacle. By the grave of St. Bona I await thee.

Come, my love, chosen of the sun, come with thy rays over-
shadowing the moon. – Song of Songs.

Such was the letter of Frumentius. Today when writing to a
woman we borrow from Foscolo or Sand, but the early poets
copied from the Psalms and the prophets so that their letters were
always burning like the lips of the Sulamites and the sands of the
desert.

About five in the evening, when the bell called all the other
virgins to prayer Joanna, holding her sandals in her right hand and
pressing her heart with her left in order to still its throbbing,
descended the nunnery stairs as quietly as a snake through grass.
The moon, that faithful lamp of the smuggler and adulteress,
which the poets euphemistically call 'chaste' and 'shy' – like the
Erinnes – rose soon behind the rampart of the convent and lighted
the path of our runaway heroine who hurried to the meeting care-
lessly trampling underfoot the cabbages and leeks in the vegetable
garden. After an hour's walk she arrived at the cemetery, a spot so
densely shadowed by cypress and fern that neither wind nor sun
could penetrate the intense gloom of this refectory for worms.
Frumentius had tied his ass to the branch of a tree which over-
topped the grave of St. Bona upon which he was sitting, holding
up a horn lantern on the end of his staff, to act, as it were, as a
lighthouse for his beloved. As soon as he caught sight of Joanna
advancing timidly among the graves he rushed at her like a
Capuchin to a ham at the end of Lent. But the place was not a propitious one for such greetings as they were to exchange so, hanging the lantern round the ass's neck, and mounting with Joanna
before him, they hastened away from those funereal glooms. The
miserable animal, bent under a double load, yet encouraged by the
prodding of four heels, levelled his long ears and broke into a
gallop, emitting at the same time such an earth-shaking bray of
protest that (according to a reliable synaxarist) several of the dead

virgins, believing that the Last Trump had sounded, stuck their bald heads up out of their graves.

Joanna who now had Frumentius's arms for a belt and his breast for a support, drew in the fragrance of the fields through her nose and mouth with an indescribable joy. Having passed the forest land the young couple now entered an open valley planted with barley and beans. It was here that when the sun rose some time later the young monk to protect his companion from its rays forced an eagle to spread its wings and follow in its flight the pace of the ass. Such was the wonderful power of his prayer; and such were the miracles performed in those days by Christians whose hearts were simple, whose faith was firm, and whose appeals counted for something with the Virgin. Today our erudites and sceptics of the century hold on to compasses and microscopes instead of crucifix or rosary; they certainly know how many feathers there are in the tail of each bird and how many seeds grow in the bud of a flower. But they can no longer tame the eagle with a nod or change lilies to thorns with a tear as could the wise men of the past. Yet despite their natural gifts these wise men are insulted by men like the Abbot Crélier, who call them idolaters for continuing to maintain planets like Mercury and Venus in a Christian sky; and atheists because they change the names of plants, shouting like Jeremiah 'Anathema Anathema and again Anathema to progress and the sciences!'

After four hours travelling the runaways stopped for a rest near a small lake, by the edge of which there had once been a colossal statue to Irminsul. This statue had been hurled by a breath of St. Boniface to the depths of the lake; but its early adorers, although now converted to Christianity, preserved in the deepest corners of their hearts some shadow of devotion for their drowned patron-saint of long ago. Every year they continued to offer him gifts, throwing fragments of wax candles, honeycombs, cakes and cheeses into the water, to the profound satisfaction of the fish, which had become as fat as the priests of the Syrian goddess on these offerings. Frumentius, who descended on his mother's side from the heroic warriors of Witikend, was nevertheless as profoundly superstitious as any child of Saxony, while Joanna, although a skilful theologian in theory, was always prepared, like Socrates, to concede a point in favour of contemporary prejudice. Indeed most of the Christians of the day, hovering as they did between the Saviour and their idols, resembled the old woman of Chios who devoutly lit a candle every day before the ikon of St. George, and as devoutly lit another before the Devil, saying as she did so that it was better to have friends in every camp.

So the two lovers as they knelt at the lake's margin offered up to Irminsul the remains of their breakfast, some locks of their hair, and a few mingled drops of their blood, in this way sealing their inseparable union with each other as the Doge of Venice once did his with the sea. After this ceremony Frumentius took a monk's robe from his saddle-bags and pressed it upon his sweetheart assuring her that by this means she might enter as a novice of St. Fulda. 'In this way,' added he, blushing slightly, 'we may live undisturbed in the same cell, eating from the same platter, dipping our pens in the same inkwell; whereas if they discover you to be a woman they will lock you away in the women's apartments with other nuns and I shall die at the door-post in despair!'

Joanna who considered the disguise would lay her open to the charge of profanity argued against her lover's pleadings with a text from the Scriptures. 'There shall be no garment of man placed upon woman, nor shall man take to woman's garments.' But he continued to press her, arguing with the help of Deuteronomy and the opinion of Origen that all women would anyhow be transformed into men on the Last Day. Joanna replied to this that Origen was a heretic and, moreover, a eunuch. Frumentius however reminded her of the example of St. Thecla, sister of the Apostle Paul, and of St. Margaret, St. Eugenia, St. Matrona,[17] and a host of others who had hidden their white bodies like angels' wings in the black habits of men and had acquired holiness living with monks. The youth, beauty and passion of the young man added arguments to his logic which admitted no refusal;

so that in a little while Joanna trod the commands of Moses under her little feet, and drew the habit over her dress. She also placed upon her feet those sandals which in the future the mighty ones of the earth were to kiss as they knelt before her. The transformation completed, Frumentius led her to the border of the lake once more that she might see her own reflection there.

Never before did cord encircle the waist of so charming a monk. Her face glowed in the shadow of the cowl like a pearl in its shell. Her lover knelt before her in ecstasy and with mounting admiration began to praise the beauty of his new brother in Christ with one of those mystico-anatomical hymns with which the monks of the day were wont to extol the Virgin; praising her hair, cheeks, breasts, belly, legs and feet like a horse-dealer praising his horses, or the poet P. Soutsos[18] praising his heroines.

At the end of this litany the young couple rode on once more, directing the steps of their ass towards the monastery of Fulda where Joanna was to be admitted to the flock of St. Benedict. Twelve full days they spent, passing through the whole country-side between Mosbach and Fulda, taking rest wherever they found shade, bathing in every stream, and carving their names on the trees that shaded their lovemaking. The sun's heat and that of youth, love, and above all, riding, made these frequent stops necessary. Besides Frumentius knew the detailed hagiography of these spots so he could always find some pious excuse to dismount. At one halt they might pray before the tree where St. Thecla cured the blind with a few drops of milk from her virgin breasts, at another they might feel the wish to kiss the soil upon which the blood of St. Boniface was spilt, and where from each drop sprang an anemone as from that of Adonis. Joanna would dismount, smiling at her lover's entreaties, while the shepherds and husbandmen they met would marvel at the beauty and piety of the two cowled youths; and, removing their three-cornered hats, they contended for the honour of offering them bread and cheese, beer and fruit. Sometimes in the road they met half-naked Slavines living like reeds by the edge of rivers, exacting a toll from the passer-by and sometimes throwing the recalcitrant into the water. Frumentius, however, successfully disposed of them with a text from St. Michael, which put these land-and-water bandits to flight.

One morning as the young couple lay reposing under an old oak, lying upon the amorous laurels – or rather trefoil (for in Germany laurels grow nowhere save on the heads of heroes) – they observed two women approaching. Their cheeks were painted, their feet were bound with fine chains, and their flowing disordered hair was their only covering. These were sinners whose penance was to go, naked and in chains, in solemn pilgrimage to the grave of St. Marcellinus,[19] where they would seek redemption.

These pious pilgrimages generally took place at the end of spring or the beginning of the summer when the temperature permitted such paradisical dress. Most of such Magdalenes, knowing that every stain would be washed away by the touch of the holy relics, showed little enough modesty about multiplying their sins on the road as they went. They would claim hospitality of the peasants, alms of the traveller, and these they recompensed in the coin with which the celebrated St. Mary of Egypt[20] used to defray the expenses of her journeys. Meanwhile the idyllic dress of these women simplified practical matters of communication or intercourse to the utmost degree. Now it was that these two female pilgrims, little guessing what lay under Joanna's habit, approached them and asked for alms, in return for which, they said, they would not only open the gates of paradise for them in the future but they would offer them more immediate joys in the present. Frumentius having Joanna before him like a breastplate repulsed the impertinent propositions of these two gorged sirens, treating them to the end of his cassock-cord as he drove them off; then holding his new friend firmly in his arms, he went on his way – like the ancient hermits were used to hug the cross when tempted by the demons of the flesh.

Yet these old holy men, while they turned away one terrified eye from the Evil One, fixed the other one on him, with a horror not unmixed with desire, like a hungry Jew refusing a ham. Frumentius who as a genuine product of the West made use of enjoyment as an antidote against temptation was able to turn away both eyes without any effort whatsoever. The saints, sleepless, whipped to ribbons with the taws, fasting until their mouths were filled with worms, rarely succeeded in mastering the tumult of those nights when they struggled against the pricking of the flesh, or of those days when they averted their faces from the devil in woman's form. So it was that hens and she-goats were withdrawn from the monasteries as dangerous to their unbearable chastity. The Franks, however, after a term of self-sacrifice, gave it up and appeased the legates of lubricity in order that they might, in calmness and tranquillity of spirit, concentrate upon salvation. St. Anthony quieted temptation with a cold bath. But according to the wise Archigenes temperance is itself the most violent aphrodisiac. How wise, how very wise, were the Franks, then, to outlaw such methods in the monasteries.

The sun which had shone out the longest day of the year had set when the two travellers, having skirted the group of extinct volcanoes which surrounded the monastery of St. Fulda, at last set foot on ecclesiastical ground. The night was moonless and soft and only stars were reflected in the waters of the Fulda. When they were closer to the monastery, however, they saw a red glow among the trees which might have been the reflection of a fire. Foxes, deer, and wild boars ran about in the undergrowth around them, apparently in great fear, while night birds fluttered madly as they tried to find the way back to their nests above the lovers' heads. Joanna trembled and clung to her companion while even the ass shot up its ears in fearful doubt as a soldier of the Pope does at the sound of battle. Spouts of fire, clouds of smoke, the noise of bells and voices, odours of frankincense and cooking – all these diverse things assailed the eyes, ears and nose of our heroine whose wonder and agitation grew with every step the ass took. The suppressed gaiety of Frumentius hardly calmed her;

yet to her continual questions he would only answer by laughing and kissing her.

As we unfortunately cannot reward you, female reader, in the same way, we would inform you instead that today, or rather tonight, proved to be the 24th of June, the very day on which, eight hundred years before, the head of St. John was handed to Herodias' daughter – very much as today one hands a bouquet to Esler or Taglioni. The bones of the saint, disinterred by St. Athanasius, had been carried all over the world, working miracle after miracle, as was the custom of the time. The head had been carried off to France by some French monks of Alexandria; for the Franks of the Middle Ages were as ready to steal the relics of saints as their descendants of today are to steal fragments of ancient Greek art. The finger of St. Sergius[21] or the leg of St. Febronia fetched a much higher price then than a head of Hermes or arm of Aphrodite fetches even today; so the greatly valued head of St. John, which reposed in the monastery of St. Angelis, was used to cure fevers in default of quinine. The renown of this miraculous head had gradually spread through the West so that every year bonfires were lit on this day in honour of it – much as the ancestors of these monks lit fires to honour the Palelia. The Goddess Palis had long since died but her ancient worshippers had not ceased to enjoy wine and dancing, and merry sleepless nights; and for want of gods they offered up to the long-bearded and scowling saints of the Christian pantheon all the joyful worship they had formerly given to the hilarious and beardless Olympians.

The festival was in full swing when the two travellers entered the courtyard of the monastery. Some of the monks were adding sheaves of stubble and empty barrels to the bonfire; others, lifting their habits, were jumping over the holy fire, and resorting hurriedly to a ditch full of water whenever they burnt their legs. Others danced round the fires or lay spreadeagled in the grass, dipping their fingers into the cooking-pots and their cups into the wine-jars; still others, holding up a burning brand, were racing about the garden looking for a hawk to chase away the devils, or hunting for a four leafed clover which would give the finder power over the forces of darkness for one whole night. The merry monks received their returning brother and Joanna with shouts of joy and Frumentius presented his companion to them as an orphaned relative, subject to the Duke Ansigise, who had found slavery irksome and wished to exchange it for the monastic habit.

'*Dignus, dignus est intrare in nostro sancto corpori,*' was the unanimous response of the Benedictine monks as they dragged the newly converted Joanna into the rapid measures of a circular dance which curled like a writhing snake among the fires. Thus Joanna no sooner had entered a monastery than she learned to dance. Dancing which today is forbidden as an invention of Satan was not then considered impious or irreligious; it was for them simply a prayer performed with the feet, as the psalms are with the lips. As both had been invented by David they were assumed to be as closely related as children of the same father.

The stars had burnt out in the sky and the fires were dying when at last the bell forced the intoxicated and sleeping company of the pot to forsake the dance or the wine-jar and hurry to matins. That morning, as always after festivals, the sound of throaty snoring rumbled under the dome of the church; and this was why they so often said that the monks had developed the habit, even when fully awake, of singing through their noses. This old custom, though banished by the Western Church along with the Festival of the Ass and other Gothic relics of the Middle Ages, took refuge with us where it is preserved in its original form to this day; and perhaps constitutes a reason for the gradual desertion from the Churches, the cooling of religious fervour and the diminishing offerings of alms.

Religions are like women, for neither when they are youthful need scents or fard in order to be surrounded by humble adorers who are ready, whether pagan or Christian, to lay down their lives for the beloved object. But when they age it is necessary for them to take refuge in stoles and gilded ornaments to preserve for a little while longer their depleted votaries. The Church of Rome became aware of this in time and resorted to painters and sculptors as soon as she saw the ardour of her believers beginning to cool: very much as the old woman Hera snatched the girdle of Aphrodite with which to hide her wrinkles and cover her nakedness. But the Eastern Church though far older than her sister insisted, either from poverty or pride, in trying to attract the faithful with nasal voices and squinting virgins. Devotion long ago waned yet the paintings of Raphael and the voices of the Lacordaires or the eunuchs of the pope, still draw pilgrims to the domes of St. Peter or the Pantheon, while for our part we go to Church perhaps once a year and even then close our ears to the whole business.

Immediately after matins Frumentius hastened to guide Joanna to her new cage. The monastery of Fulda was far more like a citadel than a hermitage. Towering volcanoes, whose eruptions St. Sturm had stilled with a few drops of holy water, surrounded it on every side; while the smooth-flowing river served it for a moat. The towers of this fortress were ornamented with machicolations and turrets for in those times the monks of St. Benedict enjoyed, apart from their wine and their sleep, taking part in the political battles of the age; and any power that ranged itself against them always found them well fortified behind the walls of their monastery, much as editors feel free to express themselves today because they can always take refuge behind the articles of the Constitution. It is true that the great Charles himself had somewhat tamed the habits of the impulsive brotherhood by confiscating their weapons and leaving them, as it were, only their spiritual armament; but the monasteries still wore their martial battlements.

Joanna visited the establishment starting with the rows of cells; she saw the quiet room for the novices, the refectory decorated with monstrously fashioned statues of the twelve apostles, the underground prisons where the bad monks were buried alive, and last of all the library where sixty scribes worked night and day, some of them scraping ancient parchments while others recorded on those once valuable relics the athletic feats of St. Babylas and

St. Prisca[22] instead of the labours of Hercules or Hannibal. The garden was completely neglected as the good fathers cared little enough for flowers and actually detested vegetables for taking up too much space in their stomachs, which they preferred to fill with the breasts of cooked geese and the haunches of hogs – likening them to the texts of the Scriptures in that though short they contained much substance.

Having described the fold we must now try and give some picture of the inmates. The monastic orders were so often expanded and so many names were bestowed on them – such as Theatines, Recollecti, Carmelites, Johannines, Franciscans, Capuchins, Camaldolites – their habits and ceremonies differed so often between the sandalled and the barefoot, the black robe and white, the bearded and the shaven, the myrrh-bearers and so on . . . that the Baron Born has attempted to classify them according to the system of Linnaeus for animals and plants. Thus on opening his Linnaean Monachology we find the word Benedictine measured against the following particularities: 'Face beardless, skull shaved, wears sandals, long black soutane extending below the knees, and a habit extending to the heels . . . crows three or four times every day and in the middle of the night with a hoarse voice . . . eats everything . . . seldom fasting.'

Such then were the general characteristics of the brotherhood; besides this the Benedictine monks of Germany wore scapulars of the Virgin on their cowls to keep their heads free from evil thoughts and lice; and their faces closely resembled those old palimpsests wherein the erotic verses of Anacreon and Sappho could still be dimly traced beneath the religious texts that now covered them. Four times a day the good fathers ate, using pig's fat instead of butter and their fingers instead of forks. Those who transgressed were punished by being deprived of pig's fat for some weeks, very much as communion is forbidden in such cases today. Twice a month they had themselves shaved; on Good Friday they all washed their feet, while thrice in the year the fatter of them submitted themselves to cupping in order to quieten irreligious desires – or, as some writers say, to prevent apoplexy. Most of them were ignorant though a few understood the Lord's Prayer while one or two actually knew how to write; to these last the authorities granted, as to Homer's heroes, a double ration of food and wine instead of beer. All submitted to the blessing on the Sabbath, but since it is not known for certain on which day God rested after the creation of the world, and they being fearful of falling into error, they remained idle the whole week long. In the end the constitution of these monks became so vigorous that many of them died standing up, as the Russian soldiers did; some report that it was necessary to push them before they toppled over.

The shepherd of this cowl-bearing fraternity was at that time the noted St. Rabanus, called the Black, whose opinions had more pigeon holes than could be found in a chemist's laboratory. This learned abbot had sailed the seven seas – or at least as many as there were to sail at that time – and was well grounded in all the living and dead tongues of the period; beside this he knew Astronomy, Witchcraft, the Canonical Law and Obstetrics. As for the latter he had invented a special instrument by which unborn babes could be baptised while they were still in their mothers' wombs so that in the case of miscarriage they would escape the shadowy limbo which unbaptised children share with unburied pagans on the banks of the Styx. At the time that Joanna entered the monastery, St. Rabanus, who was getting on in years and suffering from dyspepsia, was busily preoccupied with his salvation, restricting his diet to vegetables only; very much as Nebuchadnezzar became more abstemious during the latter part of his life . . . that is when he was changed into a bull. Rabanus was also engaged in composing hymns to the Cross, each one of these containing thirty verses of an equal number of letters, and cast in the shape of a cross, upon the same plan as those French poets who arranged their poems of drinking in the shape of a bottle or a barrel. Now the copying of these masterpieces required a skilled scribe and none could compete with Frumentius and his new brother John. So the old singer of the habit entrusted his poetical crosses to them, in this way fulfilling the prophecy of Frumentius when he said to Joanna 'and we shall dip our pens in the same ink-well.'

The happy lovers now resembled the lucky multitudes who have no history; the life of our two monks flowed placidly on in the shadow of the monastery like the river of Fulda under its over-shadowing and ancient poplars. Have you ever considered, my dear reader, how delightful and reassuring it must be to have one's beloved dressed in a man's clothes so that you and you alone can unveil her beauties? One would know neither jealousy nor the countless thorns of affliction which, according to St. Basil, make women such laboratories of torture. Her male dress would guard her more safely than the locks of Turkish harems or those belts of chastity with which the Italians secure their conjugal rights against intrusion. And over and above all this the face of one's beloved would not be sullied by loose glances, nor her ears by improper words, nor even her hands by forbidden touches. She would be pure and lovely as the wings of an angel: as that ideal virgin whom St. Basil dreamed of as standing, modest as a statue on the pedestal of her virginity, deaf to every questionable thought and contact. Tibullus's jealous sighs and Byron's diatribes against women would seem as meaningless to you as the lamentations of Jeremiah to one who has never had cause to lament. Such was Joanna for her Frumentius, a rose without thorns, a fish without bones, a cat without claws. Having lived from her childhood with men, she had none of those peculiarities or charming defects which make the daughters of Eve more terrifying than those sirens who turned out to be snakes from the waist downwards.

Seven years had passed since they entered the monastery of Fulda and still Fate continued to spin out the web of their golden days while their relations remained secret and unmolested as a pearl in the deepest recesses of the ocean. Nor indeed was there danger of the fraud being discovered for before the Crusades no

Frank ever took it upon himself to discover what lay concealed under the complicated tortuosities of the platonic phraseologists or the folds of a male habit. Only the barber of the monastery would sometimes jest with Brother John when he presented a beardless cheek to the razor, smooth as a lake during a calm.

But besides Joanna there was, unfortunately, another beardless monk in Fulda; a certain Father Corvinus whom everyone avoided because his surname was that of a bird of ill omen. (Corvus in Latin means 'crow'.) This unhappy Benedictine as a young man had been in love with the niece of the Bishop of Mogontia whom he served as deacon, holding up the tail of his purple robe at ceremonies and drinking the water in which his Holiness washed his hands after communion. The young girl had opened first her ears and then her bosom to the appeals of the young deacon, but her mitred guardian, who caught them one night as they were breaking the forbidden fruit from the trees of the episcopal garden, punished them. He cut off the hair of his niece and sent Corvinus to the monastery of Fulda to repent . . . after having turned him into a eunuch. During the early days the young monk mourned his loss as the daughter of Jepthah once mourned her lost virginity, but time at last healed the scars of body and mind alike so that gradually he came to despise women altogether and to urge his companions to acquire Paradise easily by undergoing the same sacrifice as he had done; much as the fox in the fable, when he had had his tail cut off, advised all the other animals to do so as well. Such was the philosophical existence the good Corvinus led, now that he had substituted the expectation of Paradise for the desire for forbidden fruit. One day however he received orders to repel the wood-lice which were attacking the Abbot's library and while there he happened upon a translation of the sermon of St. Basil[23] concerning virginity. Opening the book, in which he hoped to find further reasons for praising the All Highest (inasmuch as all possibilities of sin had been cut off from him) when he fell by chance upon the passage where the sainted Bishop of Caesaria advises the modest virgins to be on guard against 'male bodies . . . even if they are eunuchs be on guard against them.' Continuing along this line of thought he remarks that the bull whose horns are cut off remains no less horned by nature and strikes his enemies with that part of his head where the horns were before. In this way, too, the castrated, when inflamed by overpowering impressions are still able to. . . .' But here I must refer the reader to the treatise of the saint where he will read for himself the end of the sentence. According to the scholiasts, Tasso's *Jerusalem* was written on a shield. It seems to me that St. Basil's treatise of virginity must have been written on the knees of some good virgin.

That single reading completely confounded the wits of the monk who had been at peace for so long. The snakes, dragons, wolves, panthers and other animals used by the theologians to symbolise the passions all awoke at once, in a crowd, and began to roar and bite their tails in the deepest recesses of his heart, which once again, after so long, took on the semblance of a noisy zoo. Archimedes when overcome with joy shouted 'Eureka' when he had reached the solution of his problem. Our poor Benedictine monk began to run up and down the cloisters of the monastery shouting 'I can after all' in tones of thunder. From that day forward he was afflicted by a strange monomania which neither the whip nor crusts to eat nor cold baths nor any other prescription in the monastic pharmacopoeia could cure. Wholly restored by the god-fearing eloquence of the divine St. Basil, he clutched the book in his arms day and night as a young mother holds her first-born; and whenever he saw a woman he rushed at her, like a thirsty hart to a desert spring, in order to test the truth of the saint's assertions. But the blond women of Saxony evaded him – even though castrated – in accordance with the precepts of the thoughtful Bishop of Caesaria. Yet I think that even without this counsel few of these, aware of his limitations, would have waited for him to catch them up.

Such was the one who was destined to snap the golden thread on which the friendly Moira had strung the days of the two lovers, making their life a chaplet of perfect glittering pearls. Every night Frumentius and Joanna would enter a cave close by the monastery which in ancient times had been a sanctuary to Priapus. That deity was still worshipped in Germany under the name of St. Vitus[24] though the ceremonies had not altered with the name. The lips of the Christian girls were still continually seeking from him what the immodest idolatresses of the past had sought: pleasure or the happiness of children, and the good saint, now as then, seldom turned a deaf ear to such prayers. But one must add that it was the custom always to erect his statues in the shadow of a monastery; this, as some historian acidly remarked, made quite sure of the success of the pilgrims.

In the depths of that sacred cave, behind the wooden statue of the saint the young couple had built them a nest, lined with the sweet-smelling leaves of saplings, the skins of foxes and the rich linens left as offerings by the devoted ladies of Saxony. Above their couch there hung, like stalactites, smoked tongues, hams, dried fish, leather bottles of strong Moselle wine, and other provisions on which the two youngsters refreshed themselves whenever they grew extenuated by singing hymns to St. Vitus; since the devotion of the Saint, like that of Aphrodite, cools without a gift from Demeter and Bacchus.

There they were, on that inauspicious evening, enjoying all the good things of life while their brother Corvinus, unable to find sleep which, like a wordly friend, ever forsakes the unfortunate, was wandering in the fields and repeating his troubles to the moon. But even the moon it would seem soon tired of the monotonous complaints of this unrelieved wearer of the habit and retired behind a cloud, so the admirer of St. Basil found himself soon forced to seek shelter in the shrine of St. Vitus.

The thin sandy floor which protected the bare feet of the female pilgrims muffled the sound of his steps as he advanced to the recess where the two lovers were sleeping in each others' arms and those of Morpheus. The bed chamber was softly lit by the lamp that burned before the ikon of the Christianised Priapus, and in this light Joanna, naked, seemed to be like some goddess of Olympus. So charming was the picture she made that before her even St. Amoun would have forgotten his vows, Origen his misfortunes, and Themistocles the victory of Miltiades. Father Corvinus, forgetting for his part all about the sleeping Frumentius, rushed to place at the mercy of harsh experience the physiological maxims of the bishop of Caesaria. But St. Vitus who protects the sleep of lovers resting in his shadow was not going to tolerate the pollution of his mysteries by a miserable eunuch; and when he saw him lay his insolent land on his sleeping votaress, his cheeks grew red with anger like those of Loreto's Virgin when they kissed her with impious lips. His head shook in a menacing fashion while the oil in the lamp began to boil fiercely. A drop of that simmering oil fell upon the face of the sleeping Frumentius and woke him up; bounding to his feet he saw his companion still half asleep and struggling violently against the treacherous Corvinus, as if gripped by some nightmare. Frumentius, like a true descendant of Witikend, was filled with anger and consequently as violent as any German monk accustomed to using his fists in every argument, be it never so theological an affray. So without wasting time on useless explanations he knotted the rope of his cassock round his fist and began vigorously to thrash the wretched Corvinus across the back. Meanwhile Joanna got to her feet and hurried to hide the cause of the trouble under her robes while the two monks engaged each other with their fists and blood began to flow, though luckily only from the nose. After a determined struggle Corvinus, who had been thoroughly beaten by his infuriated rival, suddenly made off, leaving a part of his cowl in Frumentius' hands as booty: very much as Joseph left a piece of his mantle to Potiphar's wife . . . though the resemblance between Corvinus and Jacob's son ends there, I think.

Left alone once more the two lovers stared at one another in wide-eyed anguish, for it seemed quite clear that the satyr they had repulsed would not waste any time in betraying the secret of the cave to the others. It became clearly necessary, if they were to avoid imprisonment and bread and water, to take themselves off from that hospitable spot in which they had spent so many beautiful days in enjoyment of each other and the rich fare consumed in hallowed quiet and idleness. . . . But the passage of the years together with the luxury had diminished the sense of adventure in them both, so that they looked forward with horror to the trials and privations of a wandering life; and felt inclined to believe with St. Anthony that monks were to monasteries what the sea is to fishes, and that both die when deprived of their natural element.

It was in such anxious thoughts they were sunk when the pealing of the bell for matins reminded them how imminent was the danger. The night was dark but the stables of the monastery lay quite near where there still lived the same good ass which seven years before had carried Joanna to Fulda. This patriarch of the monastic stall, now white as snow with years, took his repose surrounded by his descendants and sheaves of grass. The runaways had soon untied him and wrapped some flax about his hooves to muffle them on the same principle as pirates who muffle their oars with cloth. They left the walls of the monastery in this manner, both fearful that their humble accomplice would wake the living with his braying as seven years before he had awoken the dead.

Part Three

'But the fact is that I have nothing plann'd
Unless it were to be a moment merry.'
BYRON *Don Juan*

DO YOU, my dear reader, like good wine? If you do, you will certainly hate the unprincipled tavern-keeper who adulterates his drink for gain with water, colouring matter, or even poison: and offers his musty or loathsome brew for thirsty lips to drink in the place of the divine nectar. Such tavern-keepers have, however, existed for centuries as the professed dispensers of the 'heart-giving wine of the true faith' as the learned Albinus once called religion. The similarity between the Christian priests and the tavern-keepers mentioned above may be traced to some synod of the ninth century so that these strictures, though perhaps not as polite as they might be, rest upon a foundation of canonical fact.

I say then that as the true wine-drinker loathes adulterators of the article, so indeed should good Christians loathe those who mix religion, for the sake of profit, with the various inventions of their shaven or sprouting heads; the miracles of ikons, pagan gods disguised as saints, genuflexions, tickets for Paradise, holy relics, rosaries – and the rest of the monkish truck which has rendered the profession of the Apostles as suspect as those of medical practitioners and the interpreters of dreams. From childhood I have always been fond of chemistry; and this book of mine is only a chemical analysis of the religious wine which the habited tavern-keepers of the Middle Ages gave the peoples of the West to drink. All troublesome insects and reptiles – snakes, wasps, mosquitoes and scorpions – become more venomous and troublesome the longer they live in the sun. Priests are to be exempted from this rule, however, for when they live in the sunless lands of the West they develop sharp claws and sharper tusks, while those of the East become gradually harmless and tame like the eels of Kopais.25 And since, like these eels, they are good neither to eat nor be eaten, it would be a pity if one were to trouble these

71

innocent heirs to the kingdom of heaven while they go about their tasks, frequently making the sign of the cross, burning incense, baptising children and listening to confessions. I say all this to you, my reader, so that you will be convinced of my orthodoxy in these matters. And now to return to our heroes.

After the death of the mighty Charles neither post-houses nor policemen were to be met with any more in Germany; and Saxon horses were every bit as fat and sluggish as they are today, so that our lovers mounted on their faithful ass were little fearful of pursuit.

The ass was one of the direct descendants of that blessed, animal which carried Jesus into Jerusalem; and on whose back, according to the great Albert, a cross was left, much as the image of the Divine Face was left imprinted in the veil of Veronica. All the descendants of this ass may be clearly distinguished by the intersecting black lines which meet in the middle of the back, and for which they earned the name 'Crusaders' during the Middle Ages. It has been definitely established that in cases of urgency they could compete with horses and coursing hounds for swiftness of movement. This particular breed was only used by abbots and prelates in Europe, where it gradually became extinct. It still thrives, however, uncrossed and vigorous in Egypt and Palestine where one can still see these creatures wearing saddles of gold embroidery and eating boiled beans from royal pots.

Such was the beast of burden upon which the two runaways travelled in comparative security; and as they journeyed onward they discussed plans innumerable for the future. In a little while the sun rose, hot and cloudless beyond the heights of Biberstein, and their spirits rose with it. They decided that they would travel round the world on their ass, demanding hospitality from the powerful, extending their fingers for the faithful to kiss, and leaving to others the graver responsibility of bringing the unbelievers to God. They accordingly began their tour by visiting Mogontia where they decided to attend the ceremony of reconciliation between Louis the Emperor and his sons. But when after a three-day trek they did finally arrive they found the city resounding to mournful psalms and mourning-bells, not to the noise of feasting and masques. Instead of the smell of roasting viands their noses became aware only of the odour of funereal frankincense. The unlucky Louis, surnamed the Pious or the Débonnaire[26] (these two adjectives were attributed to him almost as synonymous) had surrendered his soul to the Creator on the day before their arrival, repeating 'I forgive my sons as the condemned man his executioner'; and his body had now to be carried to its last resting place by four black horses. The latter which had been on short commons for several days previously travelled slowly and mournfully, like the horses of Hippolytos, between a double line of torch-bearing priests who chanted the virtues of the departed monarch. This piece of ritual was indulged in chiefly because Louis had bequeathed Sardinia, Corsica and Sicily to the Church. It is true of course that these islands, which were the property of the Saracens and the Greeks respectively, were no more his to dispose of than Cyprus or Jerusalem today is the King of Italy's. However the intention was judged as excellent and worthy of processions and incense. Frumentius and Joanna drew their cowls closely about their heads as they followed in the procession behind the body of the great ruler who by dying had started his journey down the road which, Bion says, is the easiest to find – even with the eyes shut. Later they left the mourning walls of Mogontia in silence.

With the departure of the pious Louis the air of Germany became less easy for monks to breathe, and many of them now began to emigrate – much as the gouty English began to forsake Nice after its annexation to France, saying that their doctors had ordered them to breathe Italian and not French air. The sons of Louis took up arms in order to back their claims to the patrimony of their father; the eldest, Lothair, wishing to make the Saxons sympathetic to his cause, indulged in the corruption of permitting them to raise statues to the ancestral idols – and going so far as to sanction the occasional sacrifice of some fanatical preacher or some fleshy Benedictine on the altars thereof. Some of the over-critical among the annalists have even recorded that the ungodly Lothair was responsible for the manufacture of statues to Teuton and Irminsul inside the palace, and that later on he started to send these as gifts to the Saxons and Thuringians in order to conciliate them. Even in our own age, however, the English manufacturers make a practice of sending Hindu and Australian idols, carved by the pious Puritans and Quakers, to the peoples of their colonies. These idols are generally loaded on to a boat with bales of Bibles to serve as an antidote, and both are embarked under the protection of the Union Jack.

The dissensions of Louis's heirs rapidly made Germany quite uninhabitable. The poor ass that carried our lovers was always stumbling over corpses or slipping into ponds stained with blood, while it was reduced to the meagre fare of brambles and thistles where once it had known barley meal, grass and leaves. Winter drew on, a harsh bitter Saxon winter, so cold that even the half-starved vultures, though dying of hunger, could hardly pick the flesh from the scattered corpses. The unfortunate runaways strayed in the snowy landscapes like sparrows and cursed that eunuchoid satyr whose lust had driven them from their well-feathered nest. The terror of their enemies and the severity of the cold had cooled the hospitality of the Saxons considerably, so that they found themselves knocking in vain upon the doors of farmsteads and hermitages alike. Sometimes they received no answer whatsoever, and when they did it was usually in the form of a Saxon face, blue with cold or pale with fright, which ducked for a moment out of a door, and ordered them to move on. Very rare was it to find a hand more merciful than this obliquitous head to reach them a piece of black bread or a dried fish.

Thus they wandered on for two whole months, following in the footsteps of the armies like scavenging crows in order to warm themselves by the embers of a dead fire, or to suck the bones from some abandoned camping place. And the day came when they looked almost enviously at the jackals that stripped the corpses of

Lothair's men and picked their bones: so much so that at times they were hard put to it not to provide a justification for the words of the wise Chryssipos in which he exhorted his pupils, among other things, not to treat the bodies of the dead as unlawful food if there were nothing better to hand.

Joanna endured these privations of hunger and cold without a murmur, as the camel of the desert endures heat and thirst. Neither sighs nor complaints ever crossed those pale lips: lips that so often kissed away the tears of her companion. Frumentius had many an occasion to bless the moment when the tides of life had cast up this blond pearl among women. The character of women can be compared only to that Corinthian copper which, while it contains many alloys, still retains some drops of pure gold. So it was that, fasting, shedding tears, consoling each other, and blowing on their fingernails to warm them, always heading southward like martins and chlorotic Englishwomen, that these two finally passed over the snowcapped deserts of the Bavarian Alps, sailed across Lake Constance, and found hospitality at last in the monastery of St. Gallus where the kind monks offered them asylum against the wolves and the soldiers of Lothair. The young couple prepared to set up their tutelary saint under that sacred and inaccessible roof-tree when one of the over-curious brothers happened to notice that Joanna's ears were pierced; and, troubled by this observation, he began to nurse strange suspicions and desires. The tip of a woman's ear was enough to disturb the peace of the monks of those days just as the fragrance of a woman's letter is enough today to rouse all the inhabitants of the Holy Mountain. Joanna, who feared further discoveries and importunities from the holy Father, managed to prevail upon Frumentius to leave the fold of the inquisitive Swiss on that very day.

From St. Gallus they went to Tegern, the oldest city in Switzerland, famous alike for the fortitude of its inhabitants and the strength of its brandy. Thence they travelled to Lucerne which they entered after nightfall in order the better to admire the wonderful lamp which, according to the annalists, was so bright

75

that it blotted out the stars and illuminated the ditches into which unwary travellers might easily fall. From Lucerne they went to Aventicum, the capital of the former Ellwangens, where they saw the footprints of Attila impressed on a great rock, as those of Jesus were upon the Mount of Olives; thence on to Sedunum where they found a skiff in which they sailed across the Rhodanus to Lugdunum.

This vessel belonged to some Jewish merchants who were on their way to Marseilles to sell Christian slaves to the Saracens of Spain. In those times the descendants of Israel, far from being persecuted, were extremely powerful in southern France. The Emperor borrowed large sums from them daily and paid the interest on his debts by allowing them to proselytise his subjects: just as we today tolerate Sisters of Mercy, the Bible Society's tracts, the visions of Agathangelus, the golden promises and all the other truck foisted upon us by our three Great Guarantors,[27] Russia, England and France. The Jews of Lugdunum employed the decrees they bought from the Emperor like so many sets of teeth with which to devour the Christians. They killed their swine, stole their children, forced their slaves to observe Saturday as a holy day and to work on Sunday, sold the recalcitrant as slaves, baptised their offspring willy nilly – and even occasionally went so far as to baptise the concubines of resident bishops. These unfortunates sent petition after petition to the Emperor; the Jews countered with purse after purse of gold pieces. The monarch did not even bother to answer the petitions; he sent his troops to guard the homes of the Jews and compel the Christians to pay the debts incurred. In this they followed the same office of the Christian policemen who today imprison the debtors of the Jews. Unjust is the accusation that this century is more covetous than past ones. From the very beginning gold has been the most sought-after god upon the earth, and its prophets have been the Jews. In the past, of course, even the Gospels were written in letters of gold in order to inspire the respect of the faithful.

Among the passengers on the boat was an old rabbi named

Isahar who in order to kill time on the voyage undertook the proselytisation of the two young monks. This completely unprincipled old moneybag even tried to take their souls from them instead of the fare for the journey. He began by giving them an outline of the talmudic myths, according to which Jesus was simply a clever sorcerer who, taught a sort of bogus thaumaturgy by someone called John the Baptist, had promised the Emperor Tiberius's daughter to make her a mother without male interference. The girl, following his directions, succeeded only in giving birth to a large stone, which so enraged her father that he ordered Pilate to crucify this fraudulent teacher of magic. According to this version the body of Jesus was later buried near the aqueduct and was washed out one night when it overflowed giving rise in this manner to the Nazarene beliefs concerning the resurrection.

After the scurrilous old man had recounted this and many other blasphemous stories to them he began to weave a verbal crown of clouds and stars around his conception of the God of Israel. He described Him as seated upon a chariot drawn by four panthers (as Bacchus was) while He held a trumpet a thousand cubits long in His right hand through which He announced His commandments to the prophets. This God also brought forth armed demons from His head (as Zeus brought forth the panoplied Athena); He was pretty well up in the letters of the alphabet, which were winged angels, and He ground up manna with a monstrous millstone and made loaves of diaphanous bread for the inhabitants of Paradise. The young couple sometimes burst out laughing as they listened to those marvellous rabbinical stores, yet sometimes they feared lest the blasphemy of it all might sink the boat under them and drag it to the deepest gulfs of the sea. Therefore they muttered a verse of St. Medardus as an exorcism, for he, like the Poseidon of our ancestors and our own St. Nicholas, rose up when there was need and calmed the winds and waves.

By grace of the incantation and the calm weather the ship anchored the following day in Lugdunum where Agobardo,[28] the only saint of those times, then presided as bishop; he was the only man among them the hem of whose robe, I too, would like to have kissed in all respect. This man believed that since Jesus is eternal and omnipresent all those who follow his commands, whether born before his incarnation or not, were Christians and therefore the rightful heirs to the kingdom of heaven. He set himself against the rendering of homage to the sacred ikons, believing it impious to represent the immaterial Godhead in human form; and he explained that the early Christians kept pictures of Jesus and His Apostles and Martyrs, not as objects of superstitious worship but as representations of human beings they had each known and loved: as today we cherish the photographs of absent friends. The good Bishop also held it ridiculous to believe that the All-Highest dictated every word of the Scriptures, such as the apothegm to the angel concerning Balaam's ass. He tried to prevent the faithful from concerning themselves too much with genuflexions and exhorted them to give more to the poor and less to the churches; for he did think it a sin that while so many poor people were deprived of their paltry obol to buy bread, the priests should receive gold to light candles at midday in honour of their statues, or spend it in decking out their concubines.

Such Christian, or rather eternal, truths did the old priest preach to his flock; had he been preaching later he most certainly would have been burned at the stake like Huss or been thrown un-lamented and unburied upon a stony rock as Kairis[29] was. But at that time the Western priesthood was concentrated to the exclusion of everything else, on debauchery and extortion; they had yet to be seized with that later mania for misinterpreting people and sending them to the stake. And if, in the midst of the general ignorance and corruption, there arose one who was consumed by the unusual desire to live virtuously or speak rationally, the priests quickly divided his portion among themselves, and jeering at what they thought was his stupidity, conferred on him the title of Saint – a term as liberally used in those days and as easily conferred as the title of doctor is today upon the most casual practitioner.

Agobardo was one of these rare spirits, a diamond in a gravel-heap, a swan among crows, a bright light in the darkness of the ninth century, glittering like a pearl in the snout of a swine. Happening upon him, as with labour and revulsion I ploughed though the mud of that century, I felt like the weary Arab at the desert spring. I wanted to rest for a few moments in his shadow.

Frumentius went with Joanna to kiss the hands of the Bishop. The travellers of those days on arriving in a strange city sought the residence of the bishop as we today seek the consulate. There they would deliver their introductions and ask for instructions or help for the continuation of their journey, for which they usually offered in exchange some sacred relics of their country's saints. Thus came about the flourishing habit of collecting relics. Private owners worked up large collections of every country and epoch just as we collect stamps in Athens today.

Our travellers had much to ask but little to offer the good old Bishop before whom they appeared with blushes and a certain coyness; but St. Agobardo knew how to discern merit under rags as doctors and psychologists know how to judge kidneys and hearts without actually seeing them. He invited them to his frugal table and much admired the beauty of the sorely tried young couple, comparing them to Castor and Pollux for knowledge and brotherly love; and when the time came for them to leave he gave them his blessing, some good advice, a pair of new shoes each, and money for the continuation of their journey.

Sailing once more from Rhodanus after six days, the travellers arrived at Arelas, the once-famed capital of Constantine the Great, and now celebrated for its sausages and its women, the latter being indebted for their beauty (as English racehorses are) to their inter-mixture with the Arabs. The two travellers after admiring the ruins of the imperial house, the metropolis, the amphitheatre and the obelisk, felt the need for taking care of their bellies, which had been empty now for some considerable time like the temple of Athene before which they were standing at that moment. So they directed their steps to the nunnery there, which was the oldest in all France, having been established by St. Caesarius[30] in the sixth century.

It was St. Caesarius himself who, it is said, wrote in his blood the following really draconian regulations: no stranger, man or woman, was permitted entry to the nunnery and the nuns were forbidden to stick their heads through the little doors. As for any who bathed their bodies, combed their hair, showed their teeth in laughter, or let their feet dance – they were lashed with cowhide whips or else chained and thrown into the deep dungeons. But it was impossible for the voluptuous young ladies of Provence to submit for long to such laws. The miserable virgins withered for a while in the cenobium as plants do in the case of a botanist; and then one day they broke out, trampling underfoot both the ferocious canons of St. Caesarius and their aged abbess, and recovering once more with their regained liberty the old colour and vivacity. After this they were governed for the most part by their own constitutions. They erected a theatre in the nunnery, went out twice a week, and fasted only whenever they had tooth-ache. When the Pious Louis attempted to bring these strayed lambkins back under the yoke of St. Benedict they answered in full council that to nobody did they owe submission save to their abbess. As for fasts and physical privations they would be happy to observe these as much as they could, but they would not take an oath lest to the one sin they should add another and more serious one: that of perjury. Such was the state of most of the Parthenotrophea or convents in Europe at that time; Peter Damianos understandingly called them Parthenopthorea.[31]

The sun forgot, as often happens in Provence, that it was still winter and warmed the flags of the nunnery courtyard when the two travellers reached its entrance. The fair porter snored at the gate which was wide open. Our two adventurers slipped through and for some minutes wandered amongst the deserted cloisters and silent corridors, coming at last to the dormitory where, according to the custom of warm countries, the young virgins were taking their afternoon siesta.

Mat curtains protected the eyes of the sleepers from the harsh light of noon and in the penumbra of shade they cast the rows of habit-bearing Aphrodites looked ravishing. These young brides of Jesus were as various in colour and race as the inmates of any Sultan's harem. There were red-headed Swiss girls, white as the milk of their own mountain-goats and placid as the great lakes of their country; newly converted Saracens with hair as black as charcoal and as hot; rosy Galatians and mountain shepherdesses of the Pyrenees. Indeed the dormitories of the cenobium resembled those botanical gardens in which flowers of every variety, colour, scent and origin bloom in friendly loveliness together behind the glazed walls of their prison.

One of the sleeping girls, possessed by some Cyprian dream, smiled as she laid her burning cheek closer to her arm, while her heaving breast showed through the white nightdress like the moon from behind a cloud. Another, pale and frowning, seemed like a carved statue of Grief sleeping as she lay, troubled perhaps by memories of her country's shores or her mother's face. Another reached out a hand to accept the abbess's discipline; still another held out arms to her heavenly spouse. Yet the majority slept peacefully enough while some snored – but these were the old women dreaming of Paradise.

The two travellers, forgetting the pangs of their hunger, were admiring to the full these different embodiments of Morpheus, when all of a sudden the silver cock which was on the dormitory clock, crowed once in a silvery voice. The clock was a masterpiece of Arabic workmanship; it had been donated to the nunnery by a Saracen prince in return for hospitality which, said evil tongues, had rivalled the pleasures of his own palace. At the sound a multitude of black, blue, grey and brown eyes sparkled like stars in the half-light as they shook off the sleep which had closed them: and fixed themselves with curiosity upon the intruders. The nuns of that age were neither prudish nor coy; and, besides, there was nothing in the gaze of our two youths which might alarm them. On the contrary, Frumentius seemed to them as flourishing and vivid as a Holland tulip while John suggested more a meadow-violet, fragrant and modest. The virgins therefore gathered about the young monks, in their shifts, pushing and thrusting like the waves of the sea, asking them who they were and how they had managed to get into their dormitory. When their curiosity had been satisfied they made haste to satisfy the hunger of their guests, inviting them to sit down at their own refectory tables where for the first time our two children of the North tasted the sweet fruits of the Latin South – the figs and raisins about which the learned Joanna inquired, licking her lips and fingers while she did so, for all the world as if they had become lotus-fruit.

Here for three months the lovers rested among the hospitable sisters to whom their canons permitted 'gardeners and pastors to rule their souls and water their monastic gardens.' They were not to know how many misunderstandings and revolting puns this phrase engendered – at least among the enemies of the clerics: though to my innocent pen it becomes an innocent phrase. Everything went beautifully for Frumentius and Joanna at the start; both became fatter and forgot their native country under the bright Provençal sky, which even today can make Chiotes forget their own fragrant island. 'Wherever the good things are, there is home,' says Euripides. The sweet honey of the lotus springs everywhere, in truth, and is everywhere offered to the insatiable lips of mortals under its various guises: to kings, thrones; to lovers, faithful virgins; to merchants, riches; and to the artist, applause. Once upon a time the lotus grew even on the snow-clouded summits of the mountains and among the sands of the desert where the hermit went in search of holiness and the sinner sought redemption. But today the lotus has become a garden plant, common as the leek. Perhaps this is why the poets have banished it from Helicon.

We were saying then, that our two monks, living in ease and comfort once more, fattened up and lived quite happily in that female fold. But in a short time Joanna was overtaken by some unknown dreadful illness. Her cheeks became hollow, her eyes as lacklustre as the stars after dawn. Instead of eating well, she gnawed her fingernails and instead of sleeping she moaned all night. Her companion continually asked her what was the matter but she replied only with tears and reproaches; and whenever he came closer to kiss her she turned her back on him. Sometimes she sent him to Sister Martha or the holy Bathilde, or some other nun, curtly telling him to kiss them. The good Frumentius, accustomed always to obey her lightest wish, positively hurried to execute these commands, but when he returned to ask reward for his obedience the poor youth received insults instead of thanks and sharp fingernails instead of warm lips.

Having described the symptoms it is hardly necessary, I think, to name the disease. The situation of my poor heroine was indeed a pitiful one; tormented as she was by sleepless jealousy, she could not even repay her lover in kind for, in her mannish disguise, she was as weaponless as a tigress in an iron cage. Meanwhile the nuns piled conjecture on conjecture in an attempt to understand what madness had overtaken this blond and beautiful monk who not only avoided all their caresses but even became enraged with his companion if he spoke to them.

At the beginning of this century all disease was attributed to an irritation of the stomach and was cured, under the label of gastritis, by the leeches of the sanguinary Broussais. In the ninth century, however, all diseases of the soul and body were attributed to the presence of devils, against whom there was no remedy save exorcism and the touching of sacred relics of the martyrs. Theology and medicine, from which we expect to attain salvation of soul and body, are the only sciences – if they may be so called – which change their fashions as often as women's clothes. Everything that our ancestors believed we now call superstition and even the barber makes fun today of the prescriptions of Galen and Paracelsus. God alone knows what our descendants will say as they read things like the proceedings of the Paris Medical Faculties on the so-called 'coloured sweat' question, or the treatise of Pope Pius on the immaculate conception of St. Anna,[32] or of the wonders of pepsin and the miracles of the ikon of Tinos.[33]

A council was called which resolved that Brother John, in order to be cured, should visit the St. Bona cave dedicated to St. Magdalene. Here there grew a tree whose scent put devils to flight and cured the blind of the age – even as the smell of fish was considered efficacious in the time of Tobit. The good-natured Frumentius mounted his possessed companion upon the faithful ass and directed its steps towards the cave in question. From time to time he would turn and utter imprecations over his shoulder at the eunuchs and demons which kept expelling them from hospitable places, and in their virulence his curses had some of the violence of those Jesus uttered upon the head of the Jewish cobbler.

Jealousy, when it is not idiopathic or constitutional (as the hunting for offices is in Greece today) can be a terrible and disrupting disease; yet it stops the moment the cause of it is removed, just as seasickness stops when the ship reaches harbour. And so it was that the evil spirit which tormented our poor heroine was cast out the moment they had left behind those things upon which it had sharpened tooth and claw. Before they were half-way to their destination Joanna had recovered her appetite and her cheerfulness, so that there was little enough left for the saint of the shrine to do.

After three days' journey they dismounted at the foot of the mountain upon whose summit they were to seek the cave. The two monks began the laborious ascent up the steep cliff followed by their ass, while the latter, which had been fasting and hurrying since the preceding day, shook its head as if it were weary of its miserable existence. It is possible that the first ancestors of the wretched beast had rashly eaten some forbidden barley they found in a corner of Eden; and that the descendants are compelled to expiate, as we are, that ancestral offence. At last, after a two-hour climb, the three pilgrims emerged upon a plateau planted with trees, in the centre of which stood the tenebrous cave where the blond daughter of Gennesaret had mourned her sinful life for thirty years. In the middle of the cave there was a trough which had been formed by the rain of her tears; tears which were transformed into pearls and given to the poor. Near this trough rested the mortal remains of the Saint. They had been buried there by the Saints Lazarus, Trophinus and Maximinus, all monks who had sought sanctuary in France as Mazzini's supporters do today in England. A sweet-smelling evergreen shaded the tomb marking for pilgrims the place where they might kneel. Accordingly the two lovers knelt down and began in low tones to sing the canticles of that purified concubine whose sins had made more sinners out of women than ever her repentance had kept them chaste by its example. We are all anxious to imitate the faults of great men in some way whenever we find ourselves unable to emulate their virtues. Many become complete drunkards in order to have something in common with Alexander; the courtiers of Louis politely had their teeth removed in order to resemble the monarch as far as possible; but the faults of the lovely Magdalene attracted ten thousand times more imitators than either of these. Indeed the few true Christians that remain, keep her as an idol and pattern for their lives, biting the forbidden apples while they still have their own teeth, and later offering to God their wrinkles and wigs for the price of Paradise.

While the two pilgrims invoked the grave of the Saint the ass, which had followed them into the cave in order to escape from the hot sun, smelled the fragrant shrub growing on the grave with a gradually increasing longing. The poor brute had not tasted anything green for a long time, but having had a monastic upbringing it knew how to respect the sacred. A terrible struggle began in its heart between hunger and reverence. Its eyes became moist. Its its nostrils distended. It drooled; opening and closing its mouth as it lightly licked those scented leaves with the tip of its tongue, as a lover might caress the hands of a sleeping mistress afraid that he might wake her. In the end, however, hunger prevailed over every other feeling; and laying back its long furry ears as it always did when it was about to perform some stupidity, it gave a violent shake with its teeth to the miraculous shrub which now hung, uprooted, in its profane mouth. The two lovers, suddenly observing their altar snatched away from under their eyes, converged upon the sacrilegious beast of burden; but they were terrified to notice the copious flow of what appeared to be blood from the roots of the plant and to hear a voice from the torn earth sighing and moaning and exclaiming: 'From my heart and not from a senseless stem flows this blood. Curst be you who wrings it. You shall bend under heavy loads and endure beatings throughout your life.' All this the female voice repeated to the appalled and gluttonous ass, and from that day forward all asses are subject, as the Jews are, to a double curse. Both are scattered over the wide world, spat upon, beaten and abused, and both are expiating not only original sin but also the secondary sins of deicide and sacrilegious greediness. The ass who was responsible for this second fall was, however, less lucky than Adam for it was given no time to digest the forbidden fruit. It was immediately seized by a convulsion and threw up its demon incontinently. Since that day the blind, the lame, the possessed, and those Provençal paralytics who were used formerly to seek a cure in the holy shrub of Magdalene, came in pilgrimage every year to the place where the bones of the destructive brute lay and heaped curses innumerable on its memory and on its progeny.

Our two pilgrims, whose hair had risen on their scalps with horror and whose teeth had begun to chatter like Spanish castanets, now ran breathlessly down the mountain and did not stop until they saw far off the azure of the Mediterranean water. Then they rested for a while under the pine trees before they began their all night march for Toulon, their ears still reverberating with the curses of Magdalene upon the ass, and with the dying groans of the unlucky beast of burden.

The port of Toulon was deserted save for a single Venetian galley. This had been chartered to carry the remains and the holograph testament of St. Mark from Alexandria to Venice. From

Venice the boat was to journey to the shores of Provence to buy slaves which it would later exchange in the ports of the Orient against frankincense, cotton and sacred relics. This period was the slave trade's Age of Gold. Venetians, Amalfians, Pisans and Genoese ranged up and down the Mediterranean like sharks, competing in the purchase of human souls from the captains of guerrilla bands and brigands who, after the death of Charles, ravaged the whole of France and Italy, pursuing their profession free and unmolested. But they, unlike those others who followed the same profession a few years ago in Attica, instead of robbing their relatives doubly by demanding ransoms, would light fires on the seashore to signal to the slave dealers to whom the captives were immediately sold, thus advantaging rather than ruining their heirs. The priests sometimes anathematised those who followed this trade, but more often they accepted gold bezants from them, not to mention embroidered vestments, rare spices, crosses set with precious stones and other products of the industry. Indeed some evil tongues have remarked that many of the officials of the papal court – the Grand Marshal or ceremonarian himself has been named in this context – entered into secret pacts with the brigands in order to enrich and embellish the Church.

At all events the galley was ready to set sail, and on the mole a skiff waited for the owner to come. He had gone up for a final chat with his Jewish agent about making up the lading. After a little while this distinguished old sailor appeared, followed by eight of his men. In his right hand he held a rawhide whip. In his left he held the end of a rope upon which, knotted up in couples like ringdoves, he dragged some newly bought slaves, sixteen in number. They numbered nine human beings and even women. (I say 'human beings' and not 'men' advisedly, for at that time it was still a disputed point whether or not women belonged to the human race at all. Those who inclined to deprive them of this right were fond of alluding to those whose love-making in Egypt was ram-like, or those no less curious equestrian lovers of Thessaly, the opinions of Aristotle, the malice of women in general, the daughter of Aristoxenos who was born with donkey's hooves, and the verse of Tobit.)

The captain was a Ragusan fisherman and had been a pagan in his youth. On being initiated into the mysteries of the true Faith, however, he felt predisposed to imitate the Apostle and become, like him, a 'fisher of men'; of human beings who could be hooked and sold in bulk like fish. Catching sight of the two lovers, who had tightened their cassock-cords from hunger as they sat dejectedly on the edge of the wharf, he thought it would be rather a good idea to ship the two followers of St. Benedict with the rest; they would be of use in assisting the hangman to maintain order among the prisoners, for they could threaten the discontented with the fires of Hell while he threatened them with the gallows. This old sea captain, though born to salt water, was also something of a politician; he had grasped the fact that only with hangmen and priests do human beings become a docile herd and offer their backs without protest to the shears. The unfortunate adolescents having tasted every bitterness that land could offer, willingly accepted the proposal of the slave-dealer, hoping to find at last some sort of rest upon the waves like Noah in his Ark: into which, you will recall, no evil thing was allowed to enter, with the possible exception of tigers, reptiles, scorpions and lice (for many of the latter were found, it is said, in the Patriarch's beard). In the meantime the oars bit into the sea and in a short time sailors, captain, slaves and passengers stepped aboard the *Saint Burchard*, such being the name of the pious vessel.

The two lovers seated themselves upon a coil of ropes near the forecastle and gazed out at the receding shores of green Provence. Jealousy had *reawakened* Joanna's love, and her caprices had increased Frumentius's affection for her. So, snuggled together, they enjoyed the pleasures of reconciliation, and indulged in numberless plans for their future life. The boat was due to sail for Alexandria but they intended to go to Athens and build themselves a hermitage among the columns of the Parthenon and the laurels of Illyssos. The adopted father of Joanna who, as we remarked elsewhere, was of Greek descent, had taught his wife's daughter the history and language of his ancestors. So now the small feet of our heroine ached to set foot on that earth which covered the ashes of Pericles and Aspasia.

Meanwhile the ship skirted the rocky coastline of Santa Margareta. The day was warm, the sea unruffled. Snowy cranes flew in the lucid sky and the sun glittered behind fleecy cirrus like the face of a young Turkish woman half hidden in her yashmak. Nothing can be sweeter in such weather than to find oneself lying on the deck of a swiftly travelling ship passing the time between breakfast and dinner with your head in your beloved's lap; sharing her admiration of the beauty of earth, sky and water. In order to enjoy nature properly both stomach and heart must be at ease. Otherwise the sun looks to us – at any rate to me – like a machine for ripening melons, the moon a lantern for thieves, the trees merely so much firewood, the sea mere brine, and the whole compass of life about as unsubstantial as a pumpkin boiled in water.

After three days the ship dropped anchor in the port of Aleria, capital of Corsica, where the crew disembarked to fetch water. The monks took the opportunity to disembark too so that they might worship at the resting place of the relics renowned throughout the world. I mean of course the authentic rod of Moses; some pieces of earth from which Adam was created; a rib of the Apostle Barnabas; a vial containing a few drops of milk from the Virgin's breast; a piece of cloth woven by her own hands; and some other no less sacred and authentic antiquities which the high-minded traveller can worship even today. On the day following, the wind started up in some force and took them past Sardinia which is famous, say the poets, for its cheeses and the treachery of its inhabitants, and the third day it fell again. . . . But really I, a poor swimmer, cannot hope to follow in the wake of my heroine's swift ship as comfortably as I once followed in the steps of her ass. And besides this: nautical descriptions of the waves, the rigging, the pitch, the shipwreck and so on, are liable to induce nausea in the reader, so often has it been done before; except when a pleasant episode about starvation or anthropophagy is stealthily introduced into the text. Hence referring all land-lubbers with unstable stomachs to the milk-and-water descriptions of the poet P. Soutsos (where hardly a poetic ruffle stirs the 'silent beach, all smiling milk') we may make so bold as to inform the rest of our readers that hero and heroine yawned, retched, were seasick, found their sea-legs – and in general endured everything that sea-farers usually endure. After a journey of two months they arrived at Corinth and started out for Athens overland, passing by Megara, and allowing themselves to be guided along the road by a young Greek slave called Theonas.

The sun swept up behind Hymettus, glittering and cloudless like the sun which first ripened the apples of Eden, as the three travellers entered the city of Adrian without turning aside to see the Pœcile. The churches were crowded with Athenian wor-shippers celebrating the Orthodox Sunday and the dedication of the holy ikons. They entered the Theseum which in those days was a Christian church dedicated to St. George. If Christianity suffocated paganism, at any rate the innocent victim made his murderer his heir, bequeathing temples, ceremonies, sacrifices, augurs, priests and dream-interpreters to the new faith. All these things the Christians appropriated and turned to their own uses, as the plagiarist does. Temples became churches; altars, sanc-tuaries; the processions, litanies; and gods, saints. Poseidon lived on as St. Nicholas. Pan was transformed into St. Demetrius, while Apollo became St. Elias. To these the priests attached long beards in order to make them more respectable: as the pimps of Rome once decked their girls out in blonde wigs in order to attract more customers. But to return to Athens. . . .

After the death of the infamous Theophilus who had cut off the hands of the painters and ordered the sacred ikons to be smeared with lime (as nurses dab aloes on their teats to make their nurse-lings feel sick): a reaction had set in among the unfortunate Easterners who had been deprived of their ikons for eleven long years now, and who felt their yearning for them doubled. So from all parts of the mountains to which they had been exiled by the oppressor there descended now a multitude of monks and painters of sacred ikons. According to some authorities not only the living gathered in the churches to be present at that joyful ceremony at which the ikons spoke aloud and the coals danced in the censers but also the dead martyrs newly risen from scattered graves. It is true of course that many violent iconoclasts reversed their allegiance when the God-condemned Theophilus was succeeded by the God-sent Theodora.[34] Parents glued their children's hair upon the images of the Virgin, monks offered their heads of hair as a sacrifice, and women scraped the paint from the ikons in order to mix it with water and drink it. Even the priests often adultered the wine of transubstantiation with the mixture. And in Athens itself, that classic seat of paganism, the fervour of the faithful became so intense that the bishop was compelled to cover the ikons with glass lest they should be literally kissed out of existence; indeed after a few days most of them had become as pale and semi-invisible as the ikon of the Saviour on the kerchief of Veronica.

According to the lawyers every transgression causes some new law to be made. In the Church of Christ every heresy eventually calls forth an orthodox dogma. The fine frenzy of the Iconoclasts created Iconolatry in which the Son became 'consubstantial with the Father' despite the Arians; while the Panagia was christened Theotokos in refutation of the blasphemies of Nestorius.[35] Pope Pius IX in order to punish the wicked doubts of his subjects on the question of the immaculate conception, established the immaculate pregnancy of her mother as an article of faith. Now who can tell what good news will spread from the blasphemous bible of M. Renan which, according to the Abbé Crélier, has already been of great benefit to religion and provided him and his companions with the means of proving truths splendid as the light of the sun?

The lovers when they entered the Theseum with their guide

could hardly find a place in the crowded church; every nook was crammed with worshippers. On that morning the service was being performed by the Bishop of Athens, Niketas, who glittered like a newly minted florin in his embroidered robes. The two children of the North were much astonished at the pomp of his attire since this servant of God was in the habit of preaching poverty to the faithful, and promising them that the streets of Paradise would be paved with gold, sapphires, emeralds and amethysts. But the prelates of those times preferred the bird in hand, and left the lice, the ragged habits and the emeralds of Paradise to those few hermits who had descended from the old Cynics; meanwhile of course they still carried out their sacred functions in those same temples where, says Plutarch, no pagan might enter and carry gold with him. During the service Theonas, who had been a curate once, bent his head and explained the intricacies of the liturgy to Joanna, pointing out that in the East the sign of the Cross was made with three fingers to symbolise the Trinity; and that one touched first the forehead in recognition of the Deity in Heaven, then the belly to show that Jesus descended into Hades, then the right shoulder because the Son was seated on the right of His Father, and finally the left shoulder in order to expel Satan from the heart. This explained, Theonas went on to name every part of the liturgist's accoutrements, describing the belt which 'girds him in power'; the knee-piece which is 'as a sword upon his thigh'; the triangular cope which symbolises Jesus Christ, the corner stone of the Church; the knife which the priest thrusts obliquely through the holy loaf to symbolise the soldier's lance which had been plunged in the side of the Saviour.

While the boy explained all these mysteries the liturgist cut a second loaf which he turned into the 'Body of the Virgin Mary' whose 'physical presence' in these mysteries was believed in by the Eastern Church of that time – especially after the day when, while the priest was chanting the *Ave Maria*, the bread had turned into a visible virgin who appeared to all holding the Son in her arms. The remaining morsels of the loaves were sanctified in the name of the Baptist, the prophets, martyrs and other saints; when these were disposed of, the living were mentioned. The archbishop, the priests, benefactors of the Church and others. And when each had received his share of the sacrific as in ancient times in the same temple they had partaken of the sacrifices to Theseus, the deacon lit his censer and shook it over the altar and the asterisk.[36] After this the 'de profundis' was sung and then . . . But it is useless I think to listen to the whole of the liturgy, for it was at Byzantine then as it is today; and so, according to the Catholics, it is destined to remain throughout the ages, as a punishment for the schism, impervious to civilisation and bound to the Gregorian model as tightly as an oyster to a rock.

The two Germans were surprised at the inordinate length of that seemingly endless service; yet it was only an epitome of the epitomes from the collection of St. Jacobus. But the descendants of Pericles also regarded the two strangers with astonishment; you would have thought they were physiologists confronted with some curious anomaly of the animal kingdom; they were unable to reconcile their monkish habit with beardless chins and cropped hair. As soon as the ceremony finished and each had received his communion bread a circle formed about the two Westerners. They were examined from the soles of their feet to the crown of their heads, while everyone asked at once where they came from, why they were beardless, and above all, why they wore drawers, a thing which to the Eastern monks represented a quite inexcusable sensuality. Joanna and Theonas were hardly able to gasp out answers for the circle grew tighter every moment and it was becoming difficult to breathe. At this point Frumentius, who had neither Greek nor much patience, was about to open a passage for them with his two fists when by a stroke of good luck the Bishop himself arrived and set them free, after scolding his flock for their troublesome importunity. Conducting them to his pontifical palanquin, which was carried by eight newly converted Bulgarians who served as pack-horses for His Holiness, he ordered them to be carried to the Bishopric which lay at the foot of the Acropolis.

Here a banquet of great sumptuousness was being prepared for the festival of the reinstated ikons.

The table was laid in the garden, under an old plane tree. It groaned under a load of decanters and dishes. The fragrance of food mingled with the odour of garden flowers. Soon after the guests began to arrive. The majority of them were orthodox monks[37] who had sought refuge in the caves and mountains during the late Iconomachy in order not to be forced by Theophilus to spit upon the holy ikons or to marry a nun in the public market place. These good hermits had all but become savages and their appearance was somewhat unkempt after so long in the wilds. Among them was Father Matthew from whose lips live worms dropped, due to excessive fasting; there was Athanasius who never washed his face or his feet and never ate a cooked meal because the temporal fires of the cookhouse reminded him so irresistibly of the inextinguishable flames of Hell. Then there was Meletius whose whole body was covered in suppurating ulcers like Job's; yet Job scratched himself with a potsherd to get some relief, whereas whenever a maggot fell from the wounds of Meletius the old man put it back again in order to miss none of the pains of the flesh and thus qualify for the rewards of heaven.

After these there came Father Paphnutius who was so deeply immersed in heavenly ecstasies and so little used to living in the material world, that he often drank the oil of his own lamp instead of water; Tryphon who never wore a clean shirt but always the unwashed ones belonging to his abbot; the hermit Nikon who had once succumbed to the sins of the flesh and had later shut himself up to repent in a charnel house for thirty years, sleeping where he stood like a horse, and eating only the herbs which grew, nourished on his tears, from the floor. After these came a collection of monks from the hills supporting their halt and quavering legs with staves. Some were like ancient chipped statues; and all without exception filthy, lice-ridden and revolting because of the mingled odour of fasting, holiness and garlic-eating which emanated from them.

The alarmed Joanna recoiled in horror from these loathsome products of Oriental fanaticism, at times holding her nose or closing her eyes, and almost refusing to believe that such human beings could really exist. Unwillingly she forced her mind to recall what she had read of cynocephalos and pithecanthropos. She remembered the passage in the Synaxaria concerning the satyrs which had lived in the desert with St. Anthony and conversed with him knowledgeably about theology. Yet these foetid and worm-eaten anatomies to whom words like pleasure and debauchery, Hell and cleanliness, were practically synonymous; these monks, I repeat, anchorites, hermits and ascetics whose memory today arouses such pity or terror in one's breast, had a tremendous vogue during the reign of the Pious Theodora; as great, indeed, as coachmen did during the time of Michael III and monkeys in the time of Pope Julius. So it was that the pious and politic Bishop Niketas was compelled to give them a reception, just as our political candidates give their hands to the rabble of the agora and the mountain robbers alike. Besides the monks he had also invited to the table two instructors in Greek, an astrologer and three eunuchs from the Byzantine court who had brought with them the imperial decree which permitted the reinstatement of the holy ikons.

When they had all taken their places and muttered the grace 'The poor eat', Niketas carved a slice of bread and offered it on a silver salver to the ikon of the Panaghia. She always received the first portion at Christian banquets, as the daughter of Rhea did in ancient times. After this the Bishop was free to attend to the wants of his guests, plunging a knife into the belly of a tender kid, from which spread the delightful scent of garlic, onion and leek, with which it had been skilfully stuffed. After they had disposed of the kid, fishes seasoned with caviare were served, and later on a whole sheep garnished with quinces and honey. Joanna who was accustomed to the plain and unseasoned meals of Germany where the banquets began and ended as they did in the Iliad with roast meat, pushed her fork with considerable hesitation into these complicated products of the Byzantine kitchen. And when she tasted the Attic wine with its blending of pitch, gypsum and resin, she turned her head away almost believing for a moment that the Athenians had given her hemlock to drink as they once had to Socrates. The monk next to her at table offered her a different glass – but this was to cause her even more distress. It was full of some monkish brew known to the faithful as 'balanion';[38] a hideous concoction still used in Greek schools where the unfortunate boarders are compelled to drink it in place of coffee. The drink itself originated with St. Anthony and was distilled from the acorns upon which pigs were fed. Joanna and Frumentius though they were seated amidst the variety and splendour of the banquet remained hungry and thirsty like the Frankish ambassadors at the feasts of Nicephorus. The hospitable Niketas noticed this and took pity on them, ordering them roast turtle doves, Hymettus honey and some pure Chios wine.

At the sight of the crimson-edged beaker of the divine beverage the good hermits were as delighted as Hades was when the Saviour descended into it; indeed everyone now began to reach out for the beaker that held the purplish nectar of Homer's birthplace. Which permits one to reflect that human nature, while it may submit for a while, like a pregnant woman to her caprice, to a misguided taste for acorns or other filth, hogs and resins, yet when confronted with the true and beautiful, regardless of its form, it positively cleaves to it. In this way did Niketas's guests also turn to the Chios wine. I begin to believe that there exists but one true and perfect taste, thus disproving the proverb '*de gustibus non est disputandum.*' When you think of it, all Adam's descendants are made from the same doughy material, eyes, ears and lips. 'For we being many are one bread and one body.'

For this reason everybody must derive equal pleasure from contemplating the virgins of Circassia, the diamonds of the Indies, the horses of the Arabians, the columns of the Parthenon, the grapes of Constantinople, the feet of young Spanish girls, ice in summer, the songs of Italy, and the wines of France. Even the

Ethiopians prefer white women to their Ethiopian womenfolk; and if in one of our churches one could suddenly see a Correggio Madonna or hear a sacred melody by Rossini or Mozart, even the most orthodox eyes and ears would turn to them. And any who still preferred those smoky Byzantine paintings and nasal cater-waulings of the litany would then be fully entitled to the name of Schismatics.

Niketas, after having given his friends plenty to drink, broke into a verse of the proverbs, 'Come drink of the wine I have mingled.' And the monks raising their glasses sang the verse of Isaiah which goes, 'Come, take up the wine and drink unto drunkenness.' But before actually drinking they piously shut their eyes in accordance with the specific decree of Solomon which prohibits wine-drinkers to look upon the wine while they drink: very much as Mohammed decreed that the Turks should not look upon their wives until they married them. If a man becomes extremely drunk it is a clear sign that he is not a regular drunkard; by the same token if a man desires many women it is a proof of great continence. So it was that the heads of these good ascetics which for so long had been full only of prayer and the intoxication of heavenly ecstasies, began now to revolve like the earth about the sun. Yet even when drunk these pious men spoke only of heavenly things. Just as old soldiers enjoy describing their battles and decorations after dinner so they began to boast of their miracles and their endeavours.

One described how, when he had been befriended by a poor man and had had nothing with which to repay him, he had planted a grain of wheat in his host's beard; so that when the good fellow shook his beard it yielded fifty sacks of wheat. Another capped this with a description of how he had once planted his wand of office in the garden of the monastery by his abbot's grave: and how in three years the wand bore him enough apples, peaches, cherries, figs and grapes upon which to feed all his brothers. Now the holy Nikon himself took up the tale and described how he had been consumed with a desire to see the glorious beauty of the Virgin herself and had fasted and prayed night and day to rid himself of this obsession. Yet the usually merciful Virgin was quite pitiless in this case and appeared before him in all her radiance and beauty, so dazzling him that he was left with only one eye: and, he added, he would have been completely blinded had he not had forethought enough to close the other eye in time.

After this recital the Holy Pangratius took the floor; he whose stick had made the stones sprout lilies. Then followed the hermit of Athenes Aegidius whose shadow cured all those who dwelt in it for a moment – so that whenever he walked the streets of a city a thousand sufferers jostled one another for a place in his shadow, as the ancients once sought the shadow of a donkey. The ascetics related these and other miracles as they drank down the good Chios wine, toasting the Orthodox believers everywhere and their dear ruler Theodora. And do not for a moment imagine, reader, that these were the mere visions of over-excited monks or even legends, for all these authentic miracles are recognised by the Church. And every Orthodox soul must, according to the law of the most holy ecumenical Synod of Nicea,[39] '*accept them in good faith with all his heart*'; and should he attempt '*to defame them as impossible or misinterpret them according to his own conceit ; anathema sit !*"

While the ascetics discoursed on miracles, Niketas engaged the two Benedictines and the Byzantine eunuchs on questions of dogma. To begin with he asked Joanna what dogma had been adopted concerning the Eucharist among the learned of the West. He wished to know if they believed that the bread and wine were actually changed into the body and blood of the Saviour; or whether they were accepted as symbol and image of the Divine Body. This question occupied the minds of the time to the exclusion of all else, like the Eastern Question today. Joanna, who was uncertain of the convictions of her host, parried this in diplomatic fashion by answering that while the sun is in the sky, its heat and light are also upon the earth; and in this sense the body of Christ may also be found in the bread and wine of Communion. This metaphorical response did not, however, satisfy Niketas who, as a disciple of the *actual presence*, was at pains to explain that the bread and wine are indeed the dead body of the Saviour and that our stomach is its grave in which it is interred by the priest: and that shortly afterwards it rises as Christ did after the crucifixion. This disposed of, Niketas went on to ask Joanna whether the Christians of the West also honoured the Virgin with the title of Theotokos or 'Deiparous';[40] Joanna replied composedly that as far as they were concerned the title 'oviparous' was used to designate chickens and 'viviparous' was used in relation to cats, so they were fearful lest these familiar words might discredit Theotokos in the sight of the faithful. It was, moreover, hardly advisable to give pagans a chance of comparing God's Mother with Rhea,[41] as the followers of Hypatia did in Egypt. Later, wishing to perplex the bishop still further, she asked him why the members of the Eastern Church did not cut off their hair as St. Paul recommends in the passage where he remarks that a man with long hair is effeminate and discreditable to the Lord. Niketas did not know how to counter this and scratched his shaggy head, returning once more to the question of dogma. He went into the doctrine of consecration, of the double nature of Jesus, touching upon the question of whether the Logos was joined to the body of the Saviour within the womb of the Virgin or after parturition – and many other such theological knots, which the good Fathers of Ephesus solved with the broadsword as Alexander did the Gordian knot; or with kicks, as asses settle their amorous quarrels.

Meanwhile night fell and the serving deacons came forward with torches in order to throw light upon the workings of the bishop's mind and prevent him from following the example of the bishops under Copronymous[42] who abolished the ikons. But the guests, exhausted after so tortuous a debate, gave up their arguing and returned to their refreshments. And Joanna, dizzy from the wine and the shouts of the monks around her – who by this time were well on the way to teaching the dishes to dance on the table and the cups to fly through the air – arose demurely and left the bishopric, to be followed at once by the faithful Frumentius.

As I have already remarked, the garden was situated at the foot of the Acropolis so that in the space of a brief climb the lovers found themselves upon the summit of that famous shrine. It was the hour when, leaving their wormy graves or the gates of Hades (now no longer guarded by Cerberus), the ghosts of the place, tympanitikoi,[43] lamias and creatures like them, walked the fields to disturb the dreams of the sheep and the kisses of lovers. But our two monks carried with them a tooth of St. Sabina which enabled them to evade all ugly encounters with these wraiths. Only at a great distance they caught sight of a herd of monsters with asses' heads who, shaking their long ears, were gazing passionately at the moon, in whose light they watched for the coming of the Messiah. Twice or thrice they stumbled against sleeping monks without waking them up: for the Greeks had by this time become quite accustomed to being trodden like grapes under the feet of foreigners.

Joanna had seen no temples beyond a few druidic obelisks and a few battered Roman ruins. The churches in her native country were rough-hewed and blockish – as were the Germans who had built them. Now she gazed with wonder and surprise at the columns of the Parthenon and the Caryatids of the Erechtheum, while the good Frumentius embraced the ankles of the latter and asked if they were not petrified angels. The temple of Parthenos Athena was called the Shrine of Parthenos Maria in those days; but on this occasion neither the nasal caterwauling of psalms nor the monotomy of church bells disturbed the rapture of the two young people. Only a few owls whose nests lay in the cracks of the roof emitted a faint whoop at intervals, as if they were lamenting the banishment of their mistress. The disc of Hecate, folded in silvery cloud, rose for an instant to shine, round and white, upon those immortal marbles – a flash of transparent brilliance such as once touched the sleeping Adonais on the mountains of Latmos. The columns of the Olympeum, the river of Ilissos, the sky-blue waves of Phaleron, the olives, oleanders, hilltops capped by churches or monuments – all these held the eyes of the young couple, encircled them like the cestus of Aphrodite itself. And their pleasure was more than doubled by their love for each other as they stood before this panorama. Indeed its beauty was more than doubled for them because they saw everything double, being drunk. Joanna sat herself down upon a marble bench and Frumentius lay at her feet, pointing out to her the little temple to the Wingless Victory and praying that their love might remain forever wingless as she. After a great deal of conversation in this vein, interrupted by kisses as authors use commas and fullstops and paragraphs, they fell asleep in each other's arms on that glittering bed of Pentelic marble.

Early the following morning they awoke and, shaking the dew out of their habits and the sleep out of their eyes, they set off down the hill to visit Athens. Joanna's heart throbbed with curiosity and fear as she realised that she was soon to stand before the many idols of that famous city; idols which Gregory had considered to be a danger to Christian souls – just as the sight of a gay and lovely former sweetheart is a danger to the man who has just married an ugly and frowning wife. But these hopes and fears were groundless. Some time before the pious Byzantine emperors had demolished the works of Myron, Alkamenes and Polykletos although these had enjoyed the esteem of St. Luke and even of Alaric. These outrages had been begun during the tenure of Constantine and continued throughout the period of Theodosius the Little.

These tireless idol breakers had demonstrated the depths of their Christian fervour not only to the bare stones but also to those unfortunates whom they suspected of pagan tendencies. The slaying of a sheep for the family feast, the placing of flowers upon a father's grave, the gathering of camomile flowers at full moon, the fumigation of houses, or the wearing of a phylactery against fever, all these things were reported by cloaked spies and were enough to damn a man as a pagan or a sorcerer. He was forthwith chained and sent to Scythopolis where the Christians had set up an abattoir. Here a conclave of pious judges assembled and argued at length upon the respective merits of the gridiron, boiling oil, and dismemberment. Countless hagiographers have recounted the struggles of the Christian martyrs, describing their wounds from which milk dripped and so on, but no one has yet undertaken the terrible tale of those who, instead of mythical milk, shed good red blood and whose wounds, far from being healed by greater fire, were charred by the flames of Christian injustice.

The two Benedictines, followed by Theonas and a multitude of Athenians, who in the days of the Apostle had 'little enough to do other than listen to whatever was new and curious,' walked all over the city. Deprived of its idols and altars Athens resembled nothing so much as a blind Polyphemus. In every niche where once a statue had stood they found a cross; instead of temples they now found small ugly domed churches resembling stone periwigs. These had been built by the Athenian Eudocia who, wishing to honour every saint with a private residence, had been compelled to undertake this horde of chapels, giving more honour, it would seem, to the industry of the beaver than to the dignity of the 'Unknown God.' At the porches of these chapels were seated the monks and anchorites of the town, scratching at old parchments or at ulcers and weaving rush baskets as they breakfasted on onions. Only the classic beauty of the Athenian girls was left for the two strangers to admire. In that age of course Athens was the harem of the Byzantine emperors. They gathered their loveliest girls from the town as later the Sultans did from Circassia. The improvement of the standard of Attic beauty began, as a matter of fact, with the Iconomachy: for when the Byzantine images were cast down the women of Athens, instead of being forced to gaze upon gaunt Panagias and rachitic saints, were able to lift their eyes to the bas reliefs of the Parthenon, and bring forth their children in their image. From this point of view, and for the good of the children, it would seem almost advisable to reform our ecclesiatical iconography – for who can deny this sort of influence, for example, in the wives of the Jewish bankers of Prussia? Their children bear so close a resemblance to King William as justly to be called his subjects; and this comes about from the incessant counting of thalers and florins bearing the stamp of the king's head.

But besides the beauty of the women our two children of the North were able also to admire the modesty of the young virgins who were wrapped in veils and who pressed close to their mothers' sides as a sword to a soldier's thigh. And these young women moreover, instead of distributing their smiles broadcast to the world like communion wafers, kept their glances upon the ground in order not to stumble, and blushed whenever the wind lifted the hem of their dresses. They differed in every respect from the young flappers one sees today, who seem so much more like married women that one wonders why their fathers are so busy seeking husbands for them.

Frumentius and Joanna continued on their way, past the old Tower of the Winds, to the market place. Here they observed with astonishment that both noblemen and bishops were gathered at the stalls buying their daily bunches of leeks. At last they arrived at the central stoa where instead of contending philosophers they saw astrologers, crystal-gazers, cheiromancers, and of course schoolmasters who had come down from their schools on Hymettus in the hope of attracting students by the sweetness of their rhetoric or the jugs of honey they carried. Teaching was so much at a discount that they could no longer keep body and soul together. Therefore they supplemented their scanty incomes by peddling the produce of their apiaries.

For ten whole days Joanna and her companion idled among the ruins, the churches, and the suburbs of Athens. For ten more days they rested under the hospitable roof of the Daphnion[44] monastery. Here the hospitable monks were prepared to offer shelter for life to the two Benedictines – whose descendants were later to expel them from their home and seize it like rapacious wolves. But the boiled vegetables, interminable prayers, straw pallets, and general filthiness of the good fathers could not long attract these children of the West who had been used, in the less austere monasteries of Germany, to well-cooked meals and regular baths. So they relinquished the glorious idea of becoming monks of the first order[45] and therefore 'angelic' followers of St. Basil; they did not even aspire to the rank of monks of the 'shorter order' for some of the rules promised to be extremely burdensome. A short distance from the monastery, however, there was a cell which had been deserted since the death of its tenant, the monk Hermylus. He was an anchorite who had decided to refuse all food save the communion bread and wine, and who had died after ten days of this diet. Here the two lovers set up a hearth and spent their small fortune in buying thick mattresses, a long roasting spit, a copper pot, a pitcher of olive-oil, two she-goats, ten chickens, and a mastiff to stand guard over all these possessions. They accepted the skull of the cell's former tenant as being a talisman of salvation inherited by them.

For the first few days in their new home the two Benedictines held an almost continuous feast. Lent came and passed, Jesus rose again from the dead, and all over the place resounded kisses and lambs grilled noisily on the turning spit. Even Nature, as if she wished to signal the resurrection of the Saviour, shook off the mantle of winter like a young widow her mourning. The laurels of Apollo bloomed, the spider-grass sprang up among the ruins, while Spring taught the asses to prance about their females. Joanna, rising at dawn, would taste the misty freshness of the coming day as she milked the she-goats. (The rule forbidding monks to drink milk, on the grounds that it inspired evil desires, had not yet been formulated.) Her milking finished, the lovely Joanna would gather the cherries which had fallen in the orchard, – by the sheer weight, it seemed, of the condensing dew on them – boil some eggs, and then waken the sleeping Frumentius. After their breakfast they would go hand in hand and fish, or set traps for hares in the grass, while the good Theonas dug in the garden. Later Joanna would retire into the far corner of the cell and get on with her copying of the lives of the saints. These she sold in the market to increase their income. At other times she read, sharing the dreams of Plato or the sighs of Theocritos in manuscripts which the monks had loaned or given her with all the disinterested generosity of the fox in the fable who gave the horse barley. In the evening supper was laid out at the door of the cell under a venerable pine tree known to the villagers as 'The Patriarch' because of its height. The produce of their garden, the fish and the hares, provided excellent fare for these two monks who, as Saxons and Benedictines, were always apt to be on the hungry side. Joanna, who read the Greek philosophers day and night – and even those records of apostolic heretics who had lived before the inventions of fasting, dogma and canticle – succeeded after a time in cleaning a good deal of the monkish rust from the surface of her mind; and being wise as well as profound, she constructed an indulgent religion of her own, resembling her fellow-countrymen of today who, because of the progress of science and the increasing number of theological schools in Berlin and Tubingen, have succeeded in evolving a Christianity minus a Christ: as cooks who can prepare garlic sauce without garlic, and P. Soutsos, Esq., who can write poems devoid of poetry. Frumentius was ready, as all heroes of romance are, to share Paradise or Hell with his beloved; he shared her chicken on Friday and her lamb on Wednesday. In Rome whenever a tyrant was thrown up, all other authority vanished. In the same way when Love becomes absolute master, every other sentiment suffers an eclipse, as the stars do when the moon rises. Zeus, they say, so far forgot himself as a divinity that he wore feathers and horns in order to please his sweethearts. Aristotle, haltered and saddled, offered his seventy-year-old back to Cleophile, whom he served as a mule in the Indies. And Frumentius now not only ate meat on a Friday, but would have eaten humble pie every day for Joanna's sake.

The smell of the kitchen scandalised the pious Greek monks not a little. Many of them, in passing the cell, made the sign of the Cross and held their noses – as Ulysses prevented his companions from hearing the songs of the sirens. Others, even more courageous, actually entered the place with the object of admonishing these two flesh-eating heretics, and threatening them with the flames of Hell. But Joanna received them so kindly, and with so much grace carved them the thickest portions, that these followers of St. Basil, 'monks of the first order,' who did not eat birds or anything that flew, except perhaps an occasional fly that fell in their soup, departed many a time with chicken in their bellies and a sin on their conscience.

It was not very long before rumours went about of the extraordinary intelligence, beauty and learning of the young Brother John; slowly the whole mountainside of hermits began to drift towards the city. Many a learned teacher of Hymettus forsook his students and his bees in order to visit our heroine and discuss the more intricate problems of dogma, or to speak of devils and divination with her. Even the learned Bishop Niketas often came and sat down under the old pine tree with them; and often, like Petrarch, he was puzzled that the fruit of knowledge could ripen so quickly in that curly head of blond hair.

But not only the priests and the learned men took to visiting her; patricians and visitors of the New Rome also began to know the road to her cell. None passed Daphnion without knocking at the door of the two Benedictines, and many of them, as they gazed at the smooth white arms or kissed the delicate fingers of Father John were seized by some inexplicable agitation, as if the devil of pleasure had nipped their hearts. Joanna, who thought her male dress a sufficient safeguard against every evil desire, and who did not yet know the morals of these Neo-Platonists, was greedy for as much of this intellectual adulation as she could get; almost every day she yoked some new worshipper to her chariot – some new adorer of wisdom and red lips. Many a time when she was surrounded by such a crowd she sighed as she thought how many more admirers she could win, and how much more fervent they would be if instead of hiding her beauty away in a habit, like a golden sword in a lead sheath, she could suddenly appear among them in a silken dress, her hair flowing about her shoulders. In the beginning Frumentius was glad of the fame that she won. But after a time he began to notice some small changes in the conduct of Joanna which alarmed him considerably. He became as worried as a coquette who notices that wrinkles are beginning to appear on her face. Now the young man despite his robust and manly figure possessed a heart as malleable as soft wax, a heart born to love as the nightingale is born to sing, or the ass to kick. So much so that while he was able to eat two hundred chestnuts at a sitting without feeling the least load on his stomach, he could not endure a single cold glance from his companion: and this, moreover, after seven years of uninterrupted conjugal love.

According to moralists, pleasure is the tomb of love. But I would prefer to compare it to the breath of the Aesopian satyr which is sometimes hot and at others cold. At any rate the kisses and caresses of Joanna had become as necessary to the good Frumentius as his daily bread; and when these flagged his appetite felt their need more keenly.

Months and even years passed, while Joanna became gradually more indifferent and the circle of her admirers widened. The sadness of the unlucky youth grew daily more marked. A pale cloud of discontent settled upon his features like a black veil over a rosebed in flower. For a considerable time he made an effort to control his despondency but finally he could not help the tears and reproaches that were dragged out of him. In the beginning Joanna sought to quieten his uneasiness by assuring him that the clouds of gloom came entirely from his own dark imaginings. But Frumentius was not to be persuaded, and women soon tire of so monotonous a melancholy as that which engulfed him. The Oceanides, although they were goddesses, only remained for one day to console the shackled Prometheus. Then they grew bored with his complaints and abandoned him to his rock where the vulture pecked out his entrails. Our heroine showed almost as little pity as they. She granted an occasional tenderness or a swift kiss to Frumentius with the air of one tossing a coin into a beggar's cap; then she would turn her back on him, at night in order to sleep, and by day in order to read or talk to her band of courtiers whose visits kept her busy from morning to night. Frumentius would usually sit in some corner of the cabin sunk in his black humour like the Homeric heroes: until he felt unable to restrain his tears or his fists a moment longer. Then he would rush from the cell and busy himself by plucking a chicken for dinner, or by picking a dandelion and puffing at it to see whether Joanna loved him or not.

But this could not go on forever. At times the young monk decided that he would cut off Joanna's head, at others he decided to run away and leave her forever. The coquetry of our heroine had indeed by this time taken on a 'more serious colour' – in the journalistic phrase. One abbot, two bishops, and the eparch of Attica already knew the secret of her habit, many others suspected the truth, while the majority still offered Brother John the incense of Platonic worship. Frumentius never for a moment ceased complaining and exhorting but she, having lost all her patience by now, gave him answers as dry as the figs of Kalamata. Their relations indeed gradually came to resemble those cacti which encircle our royal gardens, whose fruit lasts but a day and whose thorns forever. Yet whenever Frumentius managed to bring himself to contemplate leaving Joanna he felt his hair rise up in horror on his scalp. Neither with her nor without her could he live; and the miserable youth, who had yet to learn that the heart of a woman is but a quicksand, upon which one can pitch one's tent only for a night, found he had built there a home which he had hoped to inhabit for the whole of his life. Though driven forth from Eden as Adam was, with blows and kicks, he nevertheless tried again and again to re-enter that sacred enclosure where Joanna stood, as cold and malicious as the angel outside the gate. Sometimes, throwing himself at the feet of his mistress, he tried to thaw her reserve by recalling their kisses and vows, but his blandishments fell upon her cruel silences as summer rain upon dead leaves. At other times, completely despairing, he would struggle with all his heart to extirpate this consuming love, as a gardener digs up some rotten onion which has grown among his heliotropes. But its roots were deep. After such vain struggles he would resign himself to his fate and throwing himself upon the ground, bathed in perspiration, he would groan out curses upon 'the day of his birth, and the hour at which they cried, "Behold, a male".'

But do not imagine, reader, that the good Frumentius indulged himself too far in his self-pity, like the average hero of P. Soutsos, or any such biped of the romantic menagerie. On the contrary he was still the prudent, pious child of Germany, such a child as she bore before she was corrupted by the groans of Werther and the blasphemies of Strauss and Hegel. Most likely he loved Joanna as Aristippos loved Lais, as cats love milk. But he knew no other girl and in Athens it was simply not possible to find one, for the descendants of Solon were not then as civilised as they are today and mothers, husbands, brothers, and all such irritating creatures, surrounded women as thorns do roses. And these guardians had not yet reached the pitch when they would hold a candle for the enjoyment of strangers such as diplomats or admirals . . . Only the Byzantine emperors were permitted to stretch out their hands to the women – and then only the right hand. All this made Frumentius's situation an unhappy one and in some degree excused his follies, for to his flourishing and vigorous young manhood a woman was as necessary as the dew for a meadow.

The poets picture for us, in mythical countries and ages, the strange and hideous products of the vegetable or animal kingdoms: mellifluous lotuses, singing trees, winged dragons, goat-footed satyrs, hydras, giants, sirens, heroes, magi, prophets, martyrs, saints and other phenomena which none of us have ever seen save in dreams or paintings. The moral kingdom, if you will forgive the expression, also has its proper mythology, such as

109

heroic devotions, saintly ecstasies, superhuman self-sacrifies, inseparable friendships and other such tragic or romantic material. Among these chimera of past ages it is proper to place love, I think, as the troubadours of the Middle Ages and the misinterpreters of Plato understood it – though according to true philosophy love is nothing more than the 'propinquity of epidermises.'[46]

And if Frumentius was ready to make every sacrifice for the sake of her at whose feet he lay, cursing the day he had been born, it was for the same reason as Adam when he forgave his own faithless woman – because he had no other.

Yet our heroine, although she was surrounded by devotees, was not quite as well off as one might imagine. The scenes and importunities of Frumentius even while they no longer affected her deeply had the unwelcome effect of spoiling her sleep at night and her appetite for food. Even more serious than this, however, was the fact that these quarrels disclosed their secret to everyone. According to Athenaios the only two things which cannot remain hidden are love and a cough. But I (if I may be permitted a contrary opinion to those drunkards who talk philosophy at meals) think otherwise. Nothing is more easily concealed than love whenever it is happy. Only jealousy, anxiety, desperation and such qualifying things impress themselves on the face as clearly as if with an executioner's sword. But joy and happiness are given us in such niggardly degrees by the daughters of Eve that it is seldom we cannot hide them. Every woman without exception resembles those decadent but critical Romans who demanded of the wretched victim in the amphitheatre that he gratefully stretch out his neck for the sword. Joanna, with her icy thrusts, her coldness and caprices, and other feminine moods, tortured the poor Frumentius but she would fly into a rage if a cry of pain escaped him as she inflicted her cruelties, or if, in his despair, he showed a rival the door or menaced him with his fists.

In the meantime, however, the rumour of scandal at the cell began to stir up all the inhabitants of Daphnion. The sex and the indiscretions of Joanna were no longer a secret. Perhaps some even began to look upon her as a monster sent by the Franks to swallow up the Orthodox Church. Now, while it is true that many women before her, Saints Matrona, Pelagia and Macrone, wore habits, and lived among monks, yet they were most careful not to eat chickens on Fridays or sin with bishops. Among those who were most outraged by Joanna's behaviour were some 'angelic monks of the first order,' greasy and stinking like all those who are concerned with pleasing God alone. These monks had sought to ingratiate themselves with Joanna and had been dismissed with the exhortation to wash for a change and cut their long hair; it was this insult of the disdainful girl which they were now so anxious to pay back as they threw onions, curses and stones at her whenever she left her cell. A few voices were still raised in praise of the beautiful young German, but they were drowned in the general outcry.

So it was that Joanna felt herself at war with public opinion outside and Frumentius within. As she saw the fervour of her devotees decreasing daily through fear of the curses lavished on her, and the boldness of her enemies increasing, she began seriously to consider leaving Athens altogether. She had been in Athens now for eight whole years, knew all its monuments and libraries and inhabitants, and was beginning to find it as insipid as the kisses of Frumentius. And more than this she hankered for a greater stage upon which to display her loveliness and spirit. She was approaching her thirtieth year when women, not having enough of their own special defects, begin to take on ours also; by adding ambition, pedantry, drunkenness and other male vices to their feminine perfections.

Joanna was not like those Attic shepherdesses who were satisfied if Athos alone listened to their singing. On the contrary, she often shed tears upon the pages of her books as she thought that all her wisdom and liveliness might remain unknown and unsung in that remote corner of Attica. So it is that young nuns when, as they undress at night, they remember that their lily-white beauty may be seen only by the immaterial and invisible bridegroom.

This was her state of mind when one evening after bidding farewell to her friend Niketas on his return to Constantinople, she strayed along the crooked inlets of the Piraeus and saw a foreign boat enter the harbour. Its white sails seemed to her like the wings of an angel coming to rescue her from a land of exile. The boat was an Italian one belonging to the Bishop of Geneva, Guglielmo the Least, and it was journeying from the East carrying frankincense for his Beatitude and cloth of gold for his servants.

Joanna engaged the sailors in Latin when they landed and was informed that the ship left the following day for Rome. The crew seemed willing that she should travel with them and replace the priest whom they had lost during the voyage. He had been knocked down by a wave as he stood at the prow and tried, after the manner of Catholics, to quell the tempest by blessing bread and casting it over the side, and in fact doing little more than give the dolphins communion. Having agreed to the time of departure Joanna returned to Frumentius who was waiting for her in a cave on the bay of Mounekia. The weather was wet, the wind blew, and the sea groaned lugubriously beneath the cave when she entered it. Frumentius had already spread their dinner and a pallet upon the floor, and when he saw Joanna coming he hastened to light a fire so that she might dry her clothes which were wet with spray.

Although Joanna's heart had long since become hardened by coquetry and selfishness she was at this moment filled with a certain uneasiness when she realised that she was soon to be parted from this companion of hers, from whom she had not been separated for an instant for fifteen years. For a moment she almost considered taking him with her on her travels; but the troublesome jealousy of the poor monk which nourished itself upon the moth-eaten idea that women must have but one lover, as asses one saddle and nations one king, made him a tiresome appendix to carry around with her. Yet Joanna did not dare to bid him farewell lest in that lonely spot he should start weeping or using his fists once more. She therefore decided that it would be more compassionate as well as more discreet to let him fall asleep upon her breast before she left him forever. She was following, you see, the example of the Judean executioners who were in the habit of offering the condemned some stupefying drink before crucifying him. So taking his head upon her knees she began to caress his hair with her fingers and his face with her lips while the unfortunate youth, who had been so much deceived, abused and imposed on, instantly forgot all past abuses and even his beloved's treacheries. Just one touch of her hand healed all his wounds with the infallibility of the French king when he touched his scrofulous subjects. Frumentius, possessed by an indescribable joy, hardly knew which saint to thank for this sudden change, for in his extremity he had invoked them all. At last after so many sleepless nights he fell asleep upon her breast, that gentlest of pillows, promising candles and prayers to every saint he could possibly think of.

The following morning, however, when he opened his arms to embrace his beloved he found them encircling an empty mattress. It was still dark and jumping up in terror he stretched out his hands like the blinded Polypheme seeking for Odysseus. Light was still warring against the dark when the unlucky youth, bare-headed and bare-footed, came forth from the cave. Nowhere did he find a trace of Joanna. After circling the hill in vain several times, he went down to the seashore running like a wild boar from crag to crag and shouting 'Joanna' in a loud voice. The rocks threw back the echo at him and for each cry of Frumentius calling the runaway beloved, the echo seemed to repeat it a dozen times in tones of pity. The sun rose shortly upon his distracted search and he found the shore deserted. Yet out upon the sea he could just make out a rowing boat with Joanna standing up in it. Possibly the runaway saw Frumentius as he stretched out his arms to her on the shore, or dived in and started swimming after her, but she turned her face away and urged the rowers on.

The boat soon drew alongside the ship whose sails had already begun to drink in the wind and Frumentius watched it gathering way. His hopes and his strength exhausted he turned back and let himself be washed up on the shore like a wreck. When he came to his senses he thought that he had passed through some bad dream, but as the hours went by and the sun dried his clothes he realised that it was no dream at all.

For a while he thought to drown himself in the sea, as Solomon had once drowned his sorrows in wine; but the water was too shallow, and besides, he was afraid of hellfire and the long wait he would have until Joanna joined him. Then he raised his unhappy eyes to the sky above him, but no saint came down to offer him the consolation of her lips, as Bacchus came to Ariadne. Besides, Frumentius was not a woman, and who can say whether, in his grief, he would not have repulsed even Thais or the blond Magdalene?

Darkness fell once more and he returned to the cave. But he spent a wretched night on that bed where he had enjoyed the beauties of Joanna and where her memory still lingered. For fifteen days he remained in that spot asking himself, in the words of Job: 'And what light is given to those who suffer bitterness, and what life to those souls in torture?' At last his patron St. Boniface pitied him and descended from Heaven to ease his wound. One night as Frumentius, exhausted by tears, lay sleeping on the sea shore, the apostle of the Saxons slid down out of heaven and cut open the breast of the sleeping boy with a knife. He inserted his saintly fingers in the wound and pulled out the heart. This he plunged in a pit full of water which he had previously sanctified. The burning heart sizzled in the holy water like an anchovy in a frying pan. When it cooled the saint replaced it once more and, after closing the wound, he returned to Heaven.

Did it ever happen to you, my dear reader, to fall asleep with an insufferable cough and to awake and find it gone? Not expecting it to have vanished you involuntarily open your mouth prepared to pay tribute to the accursed affliction. But how happy you are when you no longer feel the tedious brute lodged in the back of your throat. Frumentius, when he opened his eyes, was prepared to pour out the customary libation of tears upon the memory of Joanna the ungrateful. But despite this anticipation his eyes remained quite dry, and this good Benedictine found that his appetite for breakfast, after so long a fast, was something stronger than his desire to weep. Shortly after this a young milkmaid passed him, carrying a pitcher of milk upon her head and a chaplet of flowers in her right hand. He called her to him and enjoyed her completely. And when Amaryllis took the copper coin from his fingers, kissed his hand, and went on her way, joining her song to the early-morning voice of the larks as the wind ruffled the folds of her dress, Frumentius stood and stared after her, realising for the first time in his life that there were other women in the world besides Joanna.

His cure may well be considered complete. By a miracle of the saint he was rescued from a silly passion, and consequently becomes useless to us from now on as the hero of this novel – though from this time forward he became a much more useful member of society. If he had been alive today, for example, he might consider himself, after such a cure, as very well adapted to practise whatever profession he wished. He could become a postman, a spy, a member of parliament, an office-hunter or a fortune-hunter; he could keep the books of some Chiote merchant, or hold the feet of a condemned man as he hung from the gallows. But at that time the singing of *Kyrie Eleison* was without doubt the most rewarding of the professions and Frumentius was very wise to remain a monk. And now I must let Joanna have a little rest before I follow her to Rome.

The great poets like Homer and P. Soutsos, Esq., write wonderful verses while they sleep; but I always wipe my nib and lay down my pen before I put my night-cap on. Only the greater spirits may be permitted expression while they sleep, but we humbler scribes must always be awake, like the Capitoline geese which woke the Romans.

Part Four

Φεῦ τῆς βροτείας, πῇ προβήσεται, Φρενός;
Τί τέρμα τόλμης καὶ θράσους γενήσεται;
EURIPIDES *Hippolyta*

THE CRADLE of every great man lies in the penumbra of doubt and darkness where only the poet or the novelist dares to move. Illumining his subject with the magic lamp of imagination he sees shadowy or faintly mocking wraiths. But when the hero reaches manhood and the blossom puts forth fruit, a swarm of historians supervene holding up the blazing torch of factual criticism. At the emergence of these forbidding torch-bearers, the golden-winged offspring of the imagination draw back in terror, for like stars and women of forty they are only at home in subdued light. And if the illumination of criticism itself becomes too bright the hero is apt to vanish in the light of his critic as Homer does in the light of Wolf, or Jesus in that of Strauss. So far Joanna has remained quite steady in her niche, quite unperturbed; but from now on she becomes an historical personage, and the imaginative chaplets which adorned the head of the seventeen-year-old girl may seem a little unsuitable for one whose head has soon to wear the triple crown of St. Peter. The materials for my story, in fact, which were taken from imagination before, are now selected from the works of eminent chroniclers! And if you find this part of my book more boring than the parts you have already read I thank you, reader, for your preference.

Rome, having failed to conquer the world by the sword, was hard at work trying to set up a cosmocracy by other means. Instead of legions she now sent dogmas to replace them in her former provinces; quietly spinning a web in which she soon hoped to entangle all the nations. At the time when our heroine arrived in Rome, Saint Leo IV[47] successor to Sergius Surnamed Pigmouth,[48] was the spider who sat at the very heart of that intricate web. Nearly every prelate of that time, whether he wanted or not, was given the title of Saint; but Leo had acquired his title in all good faith and by the sweat of his brow. It was he who had discovered the bodies of the holy martyrs Sophronius,[49] Nicostratus and Castorius, had raised with a sweep of his wand a storm at sea which scattered the Saracen fleet, had slain the dragon in the church of St. Lucia by a prayer; indeed more than once had he driven off the attacking infidels. He had also, in a manner most pleasing to God, established a monastery for women within the papal precincts where, under his protection, the chosen novices of the city were received into the church. But this great Pontiff and admirer of the Muses was a patron of letters as well as nuns. He conversed with Joanna for a whole hour, touching upon matters of weight – and several matters of less weight than substance – and was so impressed with her that he at once appointed her as instructor in theology to the school of St. Martino, where Augustine himself had once taught.

Joanna, or rather Father John (for her feminine name begins to jar upon the ear), spent her early days wandering about the Eternal City. But by that time little enough remained of the splendour that had been Rome. Lord Elgin's great exemplar Charles had already ransacked the old temples after the manner of the Franks, in order to decorate the Metropolis of Aquisgranum with the stolen columns and bas reliefs. The Christian churches built by Leo's predecessors were unbalanced and monstrously-wrought mixtures of Roman and Oriental art, very much as Western Christianity itself was at that time – in other words an inconsistent and indigestible fusion of Hebraism and idolatry. During this period nobody troubled his head much about dogma, and the ancient gods – at least as many as had not undergone the transformation into Christian saints, were banished from Olympus and had emigrated to Hades where they lived peaceably enough with the Devil of the Christians and the Satan of the Jews. The theologians recognised them as the tools of sorcerers; and it was even believed that at times they took possession of the bodies of those Christians who were known as demoniacs. On the very day of Joanna's arrival in the city some sort of ceremony was being enacted in the churches in honour of the ancient gods. Choruses of inebriated Christians were dancing and screeching out profane songs together with the cry 'Evoé . . . Evoé.' Dancers chased each other with whips as in the festivals of Kronion while the priestesses of Aphrodite dressed only in phylacteries and anklets of bells ran in and out of the crowds, offering wine and kisses to the dancers for a few coins. All this of course very much to the amazement of the newly converted foreigners in Rome, who were under the impression that all these things were somehow part of the Christian liturgy: much as those present at the more turbulent sessions of the American Congress might imagine that kicking had been accepted as an integral part of the democratic liberties.

These were the sort of people that Father John was called upon to flavour with Attic salt. During his early days he experimented on them to the extent of a few lectures on dogmatism, but his audience regarded these discussions about the physiology of the Holy Trinity, which so much exercised the Greek mind, as devoid of interest as the long beards which decorated the jawbones of the Greek priests. The successors of the divine Plato in the East were still busily discussing the true nature of God. But the descendants of Cato and Cincinnatus, being more practical, were devoting themselves to theology as a serious profession from which one's daily bread might be earned. And not only one's daily bread but ministries, bishoprics, horses, concubines and all the other good things of life which are the rewards of efficiency and practical knowledge. Instead of investigating the mysteries of the Christian heaven, these industrious and thoughtful people were busy about the extension of their dominion over the world, and the tribute that might be levied from it.

Joanna who was a clever and far-sighted young woman was quick to guess the predilections of her students. Shaking off the ideologies of Byzance she came down from Heaven to earth, from the frosty summits of metaphysics to the fat and fertile plains of canonical law. She began to discourse eloquently on the temporal power of the Pope, on the donations of Charles, on the tributes, the golden robes, and all the other sops to the ordinary people by which the Church sought to make their expectation of Paradise a little less impatient. In much the same way did the suitors of Penelope amuse themselves with the maids while awaiting the pleasure of their mistress. She succeeded at last in winning the love of her audiences by her clever tongue, as Orpheus moved the stones with his lyre. The comparison is not ill-advised for if they were not actually stones most nations were in the habit of calling them asses, and the synods 'ass-meetings.' The few instructors in Rome at that time were sent there from Ireland, Scotia and Galatia, to preach to the poor descendants of Cicero, just as today we receive ours from among the scholars of Germany.

But Claude, Dungall, Vigintimillus and all the other wise men abroad were either dead or very old by this time and, in the tremendous darkness of the Middle Ages, Italy surpassed all the nations surrounding her in sheer ignorance as did Calypso her nymphs in stature. The majority of priests did not know how to read and instead of teaching the Gospel from the pulpit they regaled the faithful with stories of how the Virgin made a habit of holding the feet of men hanging from the gallows if ever they had lit a chandle in her honour; of how she often rescued devout nuns from sin by taking their form and receiving their lovers in their stead; and how she at last smuggled them into the blessed corridors of Paradise where the merciful Theotokos mixed them love potions that they might the better enjoy their lovers . . .

In that huge darkness the knowledge of our heroine glimmered like a beacon on a foggy night. A multitude of listeners, often including Pope Leo himself, crowded the monastery of St. Martino to hear this new Augustine preaching. And instead of touching upon the fearful mysteries of religion, Joanna spoke only of pleasing and useful things – like the great virtue of the Supreme Pontiff. She disparaged the Byzantines. She explained the theories of Aristotle and described the misery of his descendants in terms of ulcers, garlic and fasts. The technique of these discourses strongly resembled that of those famous Hambourg bordels where one could find food for every palate, perfumes for every taste – and women speaking all languages and satisfying all appetites. Many a time our heroine began with 'The Judgment of God' and ended with the art of cooking. At that time, you see, the processes of the human brain had not been listed and arranged for minor talents to absorb. They had not been classified like reptiles in the bottles of a museum. Theology was literally the only science and it had, like Briareus, a hundred hands with which to draw the elements of ordinary life towards it. Everything of interest came within its scope. And our heroine had by now a comprehensive knowledge of every illegitimate branch of theology.

She taught continuously for two years and won renown for her eloquence. Nobody in Rome suspected what treasures were hidden under her habit. In that city one man's face was as smooth as another's and among monks only the nose stuck out from the folds of the cowl. Gradually becoming intoxicated with her success she half began to believe that like Tiresias she had changed her sex. Frumentius had been forgotten long ago, and still the ambitious young person in the habit was in no hurry to choose his successor. She had her mind set on higher things – like abbots' mantles, sumptered mules, bishops' mitres, and even the golden slippers of the Pope himself, they were part of her dreams. Being of a cautious nature she left the idea of a lover to wait in the wings, saving it for later like a dessert. She did not waste a moment on vain dreams but worked night and day for her own advancement, praising the powerful, teaching, writing, and composing those wonderful verses, the first of their kind in Italy, about Christ and the Pope.

She also studied medicine and according to some evil tongues she was well acquainted with the principles of witchcraft; it is said that she could force the evil spirits of the day (the former gods Bacchus, Hera, Pan and Aphrodite) to leave the gates of darkness and run to do her bidding.

In the meantime the praiseworthy Pontiff had grown very old and suffered from rheumatism. Having wanted to walk on the sea like St. Peter he had taken an involuntary bath, losing his mitre and the better part of his reputation. It was he who appointed Father John to be his 'private and secret secretary.'

There were at the papal court – apart from the Pontiff himself – a swarm of secret spies, prying officers, keyhole cooks, scurvy messengers and vile Ethiopian menials. There were also secret doors and staircases and secret rooms in the Vatican. Very often the representative of Jesus upon earth feasted at secret banquets though I do not know if he had the Apostles as companions. Our heroine, upon first entering the private rooms of his Holiness, found it difficult to get a purchase on the thick soft Oriental carpet, over which one might wish to skim like the horses of Ericthonius which when they ran scarcely brushed the tips of the flowers. When Joanna came before the Head of All Christendom he was seated on a throne of gold and ivory, surrounded by golden baskets, silver porringers, censers studded with emeralds and many other treasures. She was so dazzled by the display that she was forced to shut her eyes for a moment. She knelt piously to kiss the sandals of Leo but he raised Father John familiarly and with affection. They worked together until evening and Leo professed himself greatly pleased with her and from that day forward loved his secret secretary as he might have loved his own child.

The *cubicularis, divenderis, ostiarius, scriptoris, arcanus*[50] and the other courtiers who surrounded Leo, and were proud to serve him as slaves had once served the Roman Emperors, murmured at the beginning against this new favourite. They were as critical of Joanna as the royal guards of Catherine might have been to any young candidate who knocked upon her door. But the manners of Father John were so courteous and so affable, his disinterestedness was so obvious, that in a short time he won all hearts and everyone went to him when he had anything to ask of the Holy Father. Moreover Joanna as a foreigner in Rome had no ambitious nephews or concubines to satisfy so she was always prompt in submitting her friends' petitions to the Pontiff. The number and gratitude of these friends increased daily and in a short time the 'secret and private' secretary became a fully fledged politician, surrounded by a cloud of insatiable place-hunters, who clustered round her as chickens do round the farmer's wife when she begins to scatter the grain from her lap at sunset.

Though she was concerned for all her friends Joanna had nothing to ask for herself; or rather, she only nourished one desire. Daily she implored the merciful Pantanassa to reward the virtues of the Pope Leo very quickly by transporting him to a better life. An ungrateful and impious enough prayer to address to the Virgin . . . But in Rome the faithful are on such familiar terms with the Virgin that they not only ask her for wealth, position, horses, honours and so on; they also plead with her for the death of an enemy or a rich relation; they ask for the death of a rival in love or any other such troubling creature. It is even said they request things which would bring a blush to the sober cheeks of a pimp. At any rate assassins leave their knives upon her altars before sinking them in their victims' backs, drunkards empty jugs and bottles to her, and so on. So Joanna was naturally only following the custom of the country when she addressed her prayer to the Virgin. Yet as she did not despise the protection of the Devil as well, she frequently sought refuge in the sinister witchcraft of the time. She would call upon the spirits of hell as she drove a pin into a wax image of Leo, or raise black smoke from beneath a tripod where poisonous herbs smouldered; and the moon, which at that time made a point of listening to sorcerers, stood still as readily as the sun did for Joshua whenever she invoked it.

One does not know whether it was the Devil or the Virgin Mary who finally answered the prayers of our heroine. At any rate I am sure she did not know which to thank when Leo was suddenly taken ill one day with an illness that seemed to grow progressively worse. When the leeches had exhausted every nostrum and the priests their stocks of invocations to the Archangel

Michael, Aesculapius's successor on earth: when the Jewish sorcerers and Arabian astrologers had vainly practised their art over him for days: it was resolved by a council of bishops to have the Supreme Pontiff carried to the underground church of St. Tiburtius. There he would wait for a dream in which the Saint would reveal to him the name of a specific for his illness. In that age the faithful, when they knew not where else to turn, pinned their faith in heaven-sent dreams. Thus, though the Church burned sorcerers at the stake yet She herself practised a sort of divination by dreams, like the medical men today who persecute hypnotists but indulge in a species of hypnotism in their private practice.

The unlucky Pope was transferred from his sickbed to a black hearse which in turn was transferred by four strong priests to the subterranean church in question. Here he was laid before the altar and surrounded by burning candles, distracted doctors, and hymning monks. The great Pontiff, although a saint, was something more than merely pious, for he had spent his life in beautifying Rome, had heaped up a great treasury, built more fortresses than churches, and had defended his earthly estate against the Saracens rather than the Devil. True he had never actually burned a heretic; but he dealt with his enemies so fiercely that in every respect he merited more the title of King, as Voltaire admits, than that of Saint. And if he was sometimes called upon to perform a miracle, he did it more as a favour to his imbecilic subjects than anything else; just as Jesus felt it necessary to perform miracles for those Hebrews who lacked faith.

But sickness can transform lions into hares, and even the most sceptical man into a Christian. Byron, by far the greatest poet of this century, whose brain weighed 638 drams, has freely confessed that when he fell ill after his first phlebotomy, he felt himself capable of believing in the miracles of Moses; after the second, in the incarnation; after the third, in the immaculate conception. After the fourth phlebotomy he had reached such a pitch that he found himself grieving because there were no other beliefs of this kind to accept. The good Leo, probably a wiser man than he for his century, waited upon St. Tiburtius for a cure. For three whole days the Pontiff remained fasting and motionless, waiting for the visitation of a dream. But his pain never forsook him long enough to permit him the refreshment of sleep or dreams, so that after three days of great agony, he at last closed his eyes in that sleep which is dreamless.

After the customary rites had been performed and the body of the most exalted Leo had been washed in oils and wines, he was given over to the worms. And when the bells died away and all eyes were dry again the prelates, the lower clergy, the ambassadors of the Emperor, the notables and the burghers gathered together in the square of St. Peter to discuss the election of a successor.

In the ninth century it was not the custom to select the Pontiff in secret session of the Sacerdotal Council. There was no conclave where a horde of cardinals, locked in dark cells, voted each one for himself until forced by sheer hunger to agree to the demands of the majority. The Popes of those days were chosen in a crowded market-place with the sun at zenith and the blood and wine flowing abundantly all round, while their various factions fought out the issue with stones and bludgeons rather than with private intrigues. The Pontiff then was as much a representative of the people as were the tribunes of ancient Rome, and the people played a great part in his election. Their suffrage was openly canvassed in exchange for gold, wine, or the women who ran about in the market-place promiscuously exchanging kisses for votes. So the death of a Pope brought real joy to his subjects who, just like the man in the street under constitutional government today, had but one possession each: their vote. And in every election the merest doorkeeper has a chance of shaking the hand of the ruler, of drinking wine from his golden cup, and of enjoying the embraces of his sweet-smelling concubines. According to St. Prudentius there are days in Hades when the everlasting fires die down and the tortures of the sinner cease. Election days are like this for the peoples of the earth. Only then is it recalled that slave and tyrant are fashioned from the same common clay as the common wash-pot and the purple beaker; and that the same potter turned them both upon the wheel.

While the people of Rome crowded and jostled in the great square our heroine, who had long ago worked out her plan of campaign, stood graven upon the high terrace of the St. Martino monastery, hands crossed on her breast in the manner of Napoleon, as with eager eyes she watched the vicissitudes of the electoral struggle. There were many candidates that year for the crown. But Joanna's four hundred students, not to mention the courtiers who had received favours of her and the women who had admired her beauty and eloquence, were all stoutly for her. They praised the virtue and unselfishness of Father John, insisting that as he had neither nephews to advance nor a harem to keep up he was most likely to spend the revenue of St. Peter's among the poor. The struggle lasted for four whole hours during which Joanna grew pale and flushed by turns until at last, overcome by emotion, she sank upon a marble seat and closed her eyes, awaiting her fate. All at once she heard the great cry of her supporters mount up into the sky, hailing the new Pontiff *John VIII*. It roused her from her trembling lassitude.

The new Pope trembled with joy as she drew the purple robe about her shoulders and put on the slippers bearing the cross. As for the latter, it is not clear why they thrice came off her feet as she descended the stairway to the monastery. Perhaps they were too big. Perhaps they disliked feminine feet. At any rate a mule with a gold-edged saddle awaited her below among a crowd of cheering people. Joanna immediately mounted it and left for the Lateran where she was placed upon the throne of gold and the triple crown of Rome, the World, and Heaven, was placed upon her head, while a secretary composed the electoral decree and the multitude cheered itself hoarse. To make her triumph even more brilliant the King of England Ethelwulf arrived that day on a pilgrimage to Rome; and he asked to be the first to kiss the new

Pope's feet, and by this kiss to make all his dominions a tributary to the Holy See. He was followed by some ambassadors from Constantinople who had brought with them precious gifts and the cession of Syracuse as mementoes from the Emperor Michael. At long last Joanna saw the dream of her childhood fulfilled. Seated upon a high throne with the dense clouds of incense condensing about her she turned her radiant face upon the kneeling crowds and then raised her eyes to the sky as she exclaimed: 'Lioba, Lioba, I thank you!'

The master of ceremonies interrupted the ecstasy of the new Pontiff by inviting him to sit down upon a low stool upon which each Pope was placed after his proclamation in order to remind him that even though he bore a triple crown he was nevertheless subject to nature's viler obligations as was the least of his subjects. And while His Holiness sat there the priests chanted the 'Lord, you raise up the lowly from the mire' while they burned straw and hemp to remind him that the gilded pomps of the world were just as transient as the blaze which they kindled before him.

The ceremonies lasted eight full days. But while the old priests rubbed their mouths upon the sandals of our heroine, nature herself rose up in arms against such desecration. On the day following the coronation, although it was still midsummer, the roads of Rome were blocked by a heavy fall of snow[51] – as if the Holy City wished to proclaim her mourning by putting on the funeral shroud of winter. There were also many wonders and omens in France and Germany. Earthquakes shook the whole Empire, while in Bresse there fell a rain of blood and in Normandy a hail of dead locusts. Even the owls and night-jars which infested the roofs of the Vatican hooted for three successive nights in the most ominous manner like the geese of the Capitol did when Rome was threatened by the Gauls. I have gathered and recorded these augurs from various chroniclers in order to justify St. Peter a little, for heretics have accused him of not defending his desecrated throne by some miracle or other. The Apostle could hardly be more precise than this, especially as, according to the Sirach, *'Super mulierum bonum non est signum.'*

When after such a crowd of new sensations Joanna found herself alone at last, lying on the great papal bed, in the great chamber amidst so much silence and magnificence and odours of different kinds, she was unable to sleep although the purple canopy resembled nothing so much as an altar to Morpheus. Grief, joy and coffee have much the same effect upon the eyelids. Alexander the Great who slept so soundly on the eve of a battle whose name I forget could probably not sleep at all after the night of victory. For why should we seek sleep or dreams when the truth or the 'reality' as we call it happens to be much sweeter than either? Who can remember without emotion and longing the sleepless night he spent after winning a lottery, or receiving a laurel for a poem he wrote, or kissing his sweetheart for the first time? Joanna tossed off the gold-stitched covers of her bed and ran barefooted about the apartments. From every corner the glints of crystal, gold, blue marble and porphyry caught the beam of her candle. The papal apartments were rather like the Paradise described by St. John who, like a true Semite, aroused the cupidity of his compatriots by describing the abode of the blessed as being paved with gold and diamonds. This description contributed not a little to the spread of the Christian doctrine, for everyone naturally preferred a rich Hebrew Paradise to a poor Elysium where instead of pearls and sapphires one was to find only myrtle groves, lucid streams and gates of ivory.

Joanna, walking about the chambers, found her pleasure insatiable as she counted the diamonds and emeralds on the Virgin's statue, weighed the jewelled cups in her hands, and examined the decorations and machinery of the Arabian timepiece by her bed. Later she went to a small table which had been laid with a light dinner in case His Holiness should feel hungry during the night. She drank a glass of the sweet Vesuvian wine called *lachrymae Christae* by the pious Italians – a wine for which any true wine-lover would trade his heart's blood, drop for drop. The fumes of the wine mingling with the mounting fumes of ambition in her brain increased her sense of intoxication to the utmost pitch. If at that moment the grand marshal of the palace had appeared to summon her to sit upon the copronical chair, or the servant of Philip had said: 'Remember that thou art human also', she would have answered that they were beasts and idiots. Finding that vast apartment too narrow for one of her spiritual stature she pushed open the window, and as she stared out across sleeping Rome, she tried in vain to recall some historical figure who might be remotely compared to her. Many women before her had worn the sword or the crown. Yet in all conscience one cannot compare withered martial laurels or ephemeral kingdoms on earth to that papal authority which made one person absolute ruler by divine right over the souls and bodies of men, not to mention overseer of the World, Paradise and Hades. And who would dare to compare Semiramis, Morgana, or the Aurelian Parthenos with one such as Joanna? We have no other comparative reference to hand. Yet whenever a human being surpasses his fellows we are apt to compare him to some beast or other; to a bull if he was a great king, to an ass if he was a brave general, to a fox if he was noted as a diplomat. But what animal analogy may one seek for him who becomes a Pope?

The early morning cold and the braying of the donkeys bringing market produce into town for her subjects at last recalled Joanna to herself. Closing the window she retired to bed. That day she was awakened at ten, according to papal custom, and after washing her hands hastened to resume her regal vestments. Within the space of a few days she had mastered the art of Popery thoroughly. By the end of that week, as she sat upon the apostolic throne, the meanest person might have read upon her brow the motto: 'Thou shalt worship none other God but me.' No Pontiff before her had extended his toes to the kisses of the faithful with such exemplary humility; but Joanna, being a woman, had long ago accustomed herself to this sort of thing. Marvellous also was the ability she showed in combining worldly with spiritual authority, gathering tributes in the name of Jesus, and lives in the name of the executioner; and over and above all this, confiscating, impounding, imprisoning, and performing all the duties related to the art of government. You must not imagine, dear reader, that I set this down in any derogatory spirit. Joanna was simply submitting to the exigencies of her position with Christian patience.

Women, those incarnate combinations of love, devotedness, mercy and every other tender virtue can, when called upon to do so, positively wade in blood as in a scented bath. The Vestals, those old Roman nuns, often turned down their thumbs on a defeated fighter in the arena; St. Irene put tens of thousand of human beings to death and even blinded her son; the venerated queens, Elizabeth of England and Catherine of Russia, used the axe and the knout with the same nonchalance as they used their fans. And the Popes by divine right if not by divine order followed the same custom. St. Peter one day when hungry fell down in a trance and saw a linen cloth spread before him with all the bipeds, quadrupeds and reptiles of creation spread upon it. At the same time he heard a voice say to him: 'Rise, Peter, sacrifice and eat.' This was about the earliest revelation of their wordly authority that the Popes received, and in the times to come they rose, sacrified and ate, in order to imitate the Apostle down to the smallest detail. For by this time the rich had sold all they had and laid it at the feet of Peter, who made everyone poorer still while pretending to enrich the needy. And if in the Middle Ages they sometimes killed their fellow creatures, they did it because in those times faith in the life eternal was strong enough to dispel any remorse of conscience for those human beings they sent to the stake. And apart from this, the Popes were certain that the Apostles too would have indulged in the destruction of their fellow beings if they had had executioners and enough wood.

Joanna, according to the testimony of the historians, was a good Pope, at least in the beginning, and defended all the traditions of her predecessors, weaving at the same time her untiring web of casuistry and dogma which so skilfully concealed Heaven from the sight of the pious Christians. But scarcely anyone bothered to investigate more closely. The ancient Romans demanded of their emperors little besides bread and circuses, and their descendants made approximately the same demands on the Popes. These later circuses in Rome were, of course, devoted entirely to religion and our young heroine – or rather His Holiness Pope John VIII, being young, elegant, and a lover of pomp, made these long drawn out dramas as magnificent as was within his power to do. Day and night the smoke of incense rose to Heaven, candles burned, bells pealed, and the shouts of the multitude could be heard. Only the ladies of Rome sometimes complained that the Pontiff had not quite fulfilled his early promise, but they hoped he would soon learn to mend his ways – and deliver to them the keys of his treasury and his heart.

Our heroine remained drunk on power for the space of two years, during which time she ordained fourteen bishops, built five churches, added a new article to the Creed, wrote three books against the iconoclasts, sheared the Emperor Lothaire, crowned his successor Louis, and performed many other memorable deeds which the chronicles record with suitable admiration. Of course those historians who prefer not to believe that Joanna became Pope attribute some of these acts to her predecessor and some to her successor; or else they simply erase them altogether from the records of papal history. In the same way the Bourbonists date the reign of Louis XVIII from the day of his brother's death, omitting as unworthy of significance the rule and laurels of Napoleon. Should St. Louis's descendants predominate until the end, should they manage to hurl down all the statues of the Corsican and erase his name from every book, as the Catholics have that of Joanna, who knows whether as the years pass we may find the titan has become a legendary figure, just as we consider the titans who preceded him as mythical creatures who heaped up mountains and laid siege to Heaven?

And after a few thousand years, perhaps, when France like

Greece is reduced to a land of echoes and memories, perhaps some curious archaeologist will search for records of Napoleon as we today search for records of Joanna. He will probably inform his readers that in the dark hinterland of history there once lived a brave man called Napoleon by some and Prometheus by others who had tried to overturn kings and usurp their authority; and that as a punishment he had been nailed to a rock in the desert at the other end of the world where a hideous vulture called Hudson Lowe devoured his entrails. But let us return to Joanna.

The higher stations of society resemble mountains in that they form a cheering and harmonious sight from a distance, at times clothed in virginal cloud, or wearing a golden or purple complexion to tempt the ambitious climber thereon. But as soon as one reaches the summit, one finds oneself surrounded by thistles, thorns or wild beasts; and in the case of Attica with brigands as well. Our heroine was not long on the throne of St. Peter before the force of the analogy struck her. Day and night she found herself surrounded by flattering secretaries, place-hunters, and voracious importunates who seemed to circle round her as vultures do about carrion. She soon became bored with holding out her feet for them to stoop to and began to remember with poignant longing those honey-gold mornings when she had offered not her sandals but her red lips to Frumentius's burning kisses. Joanna now was becoming disgusted by the smell of incense: as a cook becomes disgusted by the smell of roasting quails. She found herself yawning now when she put on her gold-embroidered robes to perform some ceremony at the altar of St. Peter's; or when from the vertiginous heights of the balcony at the Vatican she blessed the people and the world.

And while the fumes of ambition were slowly dispersing, the old desires once more woke from sleep. Disasters soften a woman's heart, idleness and a good table inflame the passions as oil on a fire. It was this knowledge that caused the ancient Egyptians to limit their kings' appetites for bread, meat and sleep. They kept them up to the mark. But St. Peter's successors lived very differently, slept on swansdown, and demolished pyramids of partridges and hecatombs of venison. They changed this diet on fast days for winged fishes – that is to say geese and ducks. And in place of the apples of Eden (which the rabbis insist contain more cantharides than cores) they limited themselves to stuffed eggs, bulbs, oysters, mushrooms and other good things. All these things had by now made our heroine a model of those constitutional monarchs who, like the gods of Epicurus, snored comfortably on their high thrones and offered the fleecy backs of their subjects to the ministerial shears; like the Manichean God who surrendered the world to the discretion of Satan.

Meanwhile things in Rome were not going as well as they might have; Leo's treasuries had been eaten into, and their contents converted into chargers, ceremonies, banquets and pensions. Yet though the keepers of the Treasury had long ago emptied it they were in no hurry to surrender it. They imitated Diogenes, who when he had emptied a barrel of wine shut himself up in it. The most Serene and Holy John VIII, having become bored with affairs of states, with subjects, bulls, encyclicals and other Popish amusements, withdrew himself to Ostia which was the Corfu of the time, and there in a crowd of merry smooth-cheeked priests, he spent thoughtless days lulled by the azure waves of the Mediterranean and by the melodies of flutes, cellos, violins and lyres carried by the eunuchs who followed him everywhere.

Joanna was at the great cross-roads of her life, as Dante was when he met the lion, leopard and wolf in the forest. But she for her part felt other beasts stalking her – beasts no less terrifying to women than wolves and leopards. I refer to the approach of grey hairs and wrinkles. Her beauty, she felt, had reached its swansong. Yet although she had tasted so much forbidden fruit she still preserved her white and dazzling teeth; and her desire, which ambition had overgrown, began once more to stir in her breasts which, by the way, were as firm and beautiful as ever. Often when her handsome courtiers were gathered round her at a feast she would let her eye travel down the ranks of these habited Adonises, like Catherine going over her royal guard, and wonder to which she should award the apple, and how best she could do so. At other times, remembering the gravity of such a daring act she would recoil in fear, like a constitutional monarch before an arbitrary decree. To tell the truth Joanna cared little enough about impiety; still less was she afraid of the Heavenly Tribunal which punishes weakness with eternal fire, and boils in the same bubbling cauldron those who have caused suffering side by side with those who have caused pleasure. Having had by now a good deal of experience Joanna, who was an intelligent girl, found it hard to believe that God had placed so many good things before us simply so that we should resist them; life was not like an English banquet where the grapes which decorate the table are not to be touched. But she was afraid of scandal, pregnancy, and malice – the three guardians of female chastity. (If men were as sterile as mules and as dumb as fishes it would be a poor look-out for these three sentinels I think.)

At any rate Joanna struggled against the devil for two whole months. She spread the leaves of the agnus castus upon her bed, like the Athenians at the festivals of Demeter, or drank potions of water-lilies or lettuce heads, as Pliny advises us. She followed the prescriptions of St. John the Fasting and overlooked none of the medieval drugs which might help her stifle and suppress the youthful desires which were springing once more in her forty-year-old body like flowers on ruins. But such desires are like quicklime in that the more they are slaked the more fiercely they burn. After every victory over the flesh Joanna, instead of singing triumphal songs, found herself weeping for lost opportunities. 'One more such victory and I am lost,' Pyrrhus is reported to have said as he was counting his fallen soldiers. Joanna repeated these words to herself when, after one sleepless night, she pulled three grey hairs from her lovely head. Surely, she thought, as she saw defeat staring her in the face, surely it was useless to prolong the battle. She had already selected her conqueror. St. Leo, with his last breath, had commended to her care his only begotten son, or rather his nephew (for the children of Popes were called nephews in Rome, especially when the Popes in question happened to be saints). This youth was twenty years old at the time, blond as a Laconian dog, and absolutely devoted to Joanna. She had elevated him to the office of private chamberlain which in those days was a much sought-for title.

The name of the youth was Florus and he always slept in the room next to the apostolic chamber so that he might hasten to the Pope at the first peal of the little silver bedside bell. Joanna was accustomed, like the ancient Athenians, to carry out her decisions without delay. But now she found herself for the time being labouring under a certain embarrassment. She needed a pretext which would allow her, the Pope, to extend more than her foot to the kisses of that young innocent. Many a time at midnight, leaving her bed, she would tiptoe into the room where the chosen successor to Frumentius lay asleep. And she would gaze for hours at him, shading the lamp with her hands as Selene had once covered her beams with clouds when she visited the Latmian shepherd. One night however, she plucked up enough courage to touch his sleeping forehead with her lips; but she fled in terror when she saw his eyelids flutter. Next day the good Florus announced to his friends that a nocturnal vision dressed in a chemise had visited him while he slept. But so common were visions, ghosts and dreams in those days that most of his listeners showed no surprise, and many of them yawned in his face. Nevertheless Florus was certain that his apparition was something quite uncommon and the next night he lay trembling in bed, unable to sleep.

All was still in the papal household with the exception of the owls, and the clocks, when his ears caught a low rustle of sound, like the flight of some nocturnal bird, or the movement of some young girl hurrying to her first assignation and fearful that the sound of her footsteps might be overheard. The door opened as softly as if by a light wind and once more that apparition approached the bed, walking on tiptoe. Florus felt his nightshirt grow moist with sweat as cold as the waters of the Styx. I mean, of course, the Arcadian river and not the infernal one which was hot. The gloom increased his terror. The vision appeared to be self-illuminated and, like a ghost, carried no lamp in its hand. He could only dimly make out its shape in the light of the smouldering fire but it seemed like some white and lowering cloud as it approached the bed. At last it stood by the bed, cloud, phantom, vampire, Joanna. Encouraged by the absolute immobility of the sleeper she began very softly to nibble the soft skin of the forbidden fruit with her lips. She did not dare to bite it.

This warm contact immediately dissipated the chilly fear which had settled on the blood of the boy; as he came to himself he stretched out both arms to seize the phantom but it just succeeded in evading him and escaping. It left in his hands a torn chemise and some yellow hairs. By now the good Florus was not satisfied with these spoils. His blood was up, and so was his curiosity. He pursued the apparition which fled swiftly into the bedroom, where it proceeded to go round in a circle until at last it caught its foot in a corner of its own gown and fell full length on the floor beneath the open window. Florus stretched out his arms. Instead of encountering bones, maggots, corruption, or any other classical attribute of vampirism his hands found themselves upon a smooth warm skin which seemed to cover a living and beating heart. As he did so the moon came out from behind the clouds and shone full upon the face and the bare breasts of the Most Serene and Holy Pontiff, John VIII.

Here, my dear reader, I could if I wished borrow some timely obscenity to fatten up my story from the Abbot Casti, the most holy Pulci, or the right reverend Rabelais. The story could do with it. It has become as dry as the stricken fig-tree of the New Testament. But being neither theologian nor priest nor even an acting-deacon I do not feel that I have the right to pollute either my hands or your ears. The creator of *Don Juan* found himself in roughly the same predicament when, after a long pursuit, his hero's hand actually rested upon the white bosom of the third or fourth of his heroines – lulled as softly as the Ark on Ararat. And not being at all clear how to go on and remain his usual modest self, Byron abandoned the poem and poetry, and became in despair a misanthropist and philhellene, and took himself off to be buried in a swamp at Missolonghi. But since this is a purely factual account of events, I feel bound to confess that things went so well for Joanna and Florus after the necessary confessions and explanations that the cheeks of the Virgin which they had forgotten to cover became positively scarlet with shame. The cheeks of St. Peter turned green with rage. And the ikon of the Crucified fell down and smashed itself to pieces, while the guardian angel of Pope John VIII who had been blissfully unaware that the keeper of the heavenly keys was a woman – flew off into heaven with indignant wing-beats.

Had this abominable act been committed during the day I have no doubt but that it would have caused an eclipse of the sun. As it took place during the night, however, the chronologers have to be content with describing how a blood-stained cloud encircled the moon. According to others the omen was carried over to the following day when the inhabitants of the eternal city waited in vain for the morning star to rise. The night, indeed, was three times as long as it usually is, as was the night on which Zeus begat Hercules. But one doubts whether Joanna found it tedious if only because, in the words of Solomon, 'neither Hades nor fire nor woman's love can be quenched.'

On the morning following that three-fold night the Pope appeared before his courtiers and looked positively radiant; his lips and hands bestowed blessings and favours all around him. This papal exuberance was immediately copied by the faces of the courtiers who raised their sad heads once more like corn when the rain interrupts a long drought. The Head of All Christendom on that day alone distributed four bishoprics, ordained sixteen deacons, added two Saints to the Calendar, freed five criminals from the gallows, and rescued twenty heretics from the stake. And he still regretted that he did not have the hundred hands of

Braierus to redouble his charities. Later on Joanna took herself off to church to receive the Ambassadors of Prince Ansigese who sought her aid against the Saracens. This she granted immediately. And while she performed all these acts her eyes unconsciously sought those of Florus again and again, while his spirit fluttered about her head like a bee about a flower. She caught herself repeating like the prophet king: 'Who is it that giveth me wings to fly like unto doves, who is it that affords me rest?'

For two whole months she continued to float like a swan upon the river of inexhaustible pleasure, adored by her new lover – even though she had come to that stage in life when we usually begin to turn the pages of the book of desire backwards. Florus was at that blissful age when even the thorns seem fragrant, and when all women seem beautiful. To them we offer our hearts recklessly as gifts, to them we auction our kisses at the lightest bid. For we are like a thirsty man who is indifferent as to whether the glass he drinks is brackish or muddy so long as it allays his thirst. And although our heroine was forty she was not at all unattractive. Her teeth were still a good deal whiter than her hair. And for the velvety down and fragrance of youth nature had substituted that voluptuous plumpness, that ampleness of address which so fascinates the adolescent who is on the look-out for a skilful initiator.

A number of critics (whether orthodox or not I cannot say) prefer the Odyssey to the Iliad. There are painters who prefer ruins to habitable buildings; and there are gourmets who like their game high. On the same principle many of the followers of Solomon insist that the more mature mistresses know best how to flavour the forbidden fruit, and decorate the pathway which leads to it as Jesuits do the path to Paradise.

Petrarch in his old age pictured his ideal women as combining maturity with radiant youth and he vainly ran about among the gardens and groves hunting for this chimera which he called 'ripe fruit on a flowering tree.' But Florus was as yet out of reach of such speculations and he would not have exchanged his Joanna of forty for two twenty-year-old virgins.

The summer passed slowly, but His Holiness showed no signs of stirring. The autumn leaves piled up around the boles of the trees, the whispers of the sea changed to snarls and roars, the wolves descended from the mountains, yet despite all this the lovers remained as happy and tender as ring-doves in spring. A number of philosophers have tried to epitomise the difference between man and the beasts. The Hebrews insisted that there was no difference at all. The Christians stated that man has a soul, the philosophers described him as being a rational animal, while Aristotle said that he sneezed more frequently than other animals. But far better than all these speculations was the remark of Socrates who noted that man surpasses the animals in one thing: what they do in spring-time only the average man does all the year round. Zeus in order to justify his rather overpowering conjugal claims threw the whole blame on the spring's influence, and was most particular to see that flowers grew whenever he wanted to 'commune' with Hera. But Joanna being unable to perform this miracle substituted faggots and candles for the rays of the vernal sun, aloe and cinnamon for the fragrance of flowers, and flute music and her own clear voice for birdsong. Banquets, dicing, monkeys, mimes, jesters and other amusements followed hard on each other's heels at the papal palace. Some authorities mention also Bacchanalian chanting and the trampling noise of dancers echoing down the corridors. No longer did the Pontiff appear at matins. He followed the rule of Solomon, 'What profits it to rise early?'; and composed his own prayers, liturgies and services following the model of the Testament which forbids nonsense to Christian believers. Many a time after a marvellous, threefold night of pleasure she would tear herself from the arms of her beloved and amend the text of the Lord's Prayer to the extent of asking her heavenly father to 'grant her her daily Florus.'

Once upon a time some King of Persia, Cyrus, Cambyses, Xerxes or Chosroes – I forget exactly which one – offered a prize to anyone who could teach him a new delight. For myself I would be quite content with those that have existed since Eve's fall, but they have the drawback of not being lasting. The cup of sweetness is either out of reach when we are thirsty, or else the nectar in it is changed to vinegar all of a sudden and we avert our disgusted faces. Some such disappointment was in store for Joanna, who, all sails spread to the deep-sea winds of pleasure, was sailing along at a tremendous pace when she came unexpectedly upon a hidden reef which she had long ago given up worrying about. After so many years with Frumentius and his rivals she had come to the conclusion that forbidden fruit had no ill-effects upon her robust constitution. And since she had not opened for so long the book of the Scriptures she had doubtless forgotten that nearly all the biblical heroines, Sarah, Rebecca, Rachel and the rest, were barren until old age – when they began turning out prophets and patriarchs.

She was, therefore, extremely surprised when she noted those symptoms described in the fourth book of Aristotle which intimated (as the angel had intimated to Samson's mother) that the Dove had descended into her womb. But whereas the Hebrew woman had rejoiced at the first kick of her babe Joanna dropped the cup which she was holding to her lips and left the room in great agitation, while the guests cheered and applauded the spilling of the wine as a propitious omen. Running to her chamber she locked herself in and began to lament her evil luck.

That night long after all eyes in the Pontiff's household had been fast closed for hours Joanna, still sleepless, lay with her chin on her hands, like St. Peter after he had renounced Jesus, and vainly tried to find some way out of the dilemma. At times she considered leaving Rome altogether, abandoning the holy keys, and running away with Florus to some remote corner of the earth; at others she decided to try to dislodge the troublesome resident in her body with exorcisms or potions. But either plan presented a problem, for she wished neither to abandon the apostolic throne nor to have her life endangered. She sought in vain for some solution to the riddle. Her head was heavy, her ears buzzed, and across her field of vision there moved those sparks and lights which the Stagirite defined as certain signs of pregnancy. Suddenly there came a great noise of wings and she raised her head to see, standing before her, a white-feathered youth dressed in shimmering robes and wearing a halo about his head. In this right hand he held a red candle and in his left a cup.

Our heroine had never beheld an angel before except in ikons. She was sufficiently thrown off her balance not even to rise or offer him a chair. However the heavenly envoy, pausing only to fold back his wings into place and push his blond hair up out of his eyes, fixed a fierce glance upon the unlucky woman pope and said: ' Joanna, this candle symbolises the eternal fire of hell for your unlawfulness, while this cup symbolises premature death and disgrace upon earth. Choose between them.'

This heavenly proposition threw Joanna into confusion and she wavered for a long time like David when asked to choose between hunger, war and plague. The fear of death and the fear of Hell struggled for domination in her heart as Esau and Jacob in the womb of Rebecca. At first she held out her hand for the candle, deciding to sacrifice her future life for the sake of the present; but the spirits of the chasm which were always present at these invisible scenes, shone so brightly and delineated so much sadness on the face of the angel that, regretting her choice, she withdrew her hand again, and extended its fellow to grasp the cup of death and disgrace. This she took from him and emptied it to the dregs.

These events, good reader, are exactly as they were narrated by the chronicler. You, if you belong to that school which interprets the miracles of the Scripture as the results of natural causes, as Plato interpreted mythology, believing that the angel who handed the lily to the Virgin was really a lover in disguise, and that Lazarus was sound asleep when woken by Jesus; if, as I have said, you belong to this order you will certainly not believe that Joanna saw an angel in a dream. You will say that some facetious deacon, learning her secret, put on a pair of wings to frighten her. If you prefer the method of Strauss, however, you might spend your

141

time by calling the miracles of the Bible myths rather than try to elucidate the inexplicable. As for me, belonging to neither school, I prefer to take things as I find them; as Solomon remarked: 'The simple indeed believe every word.'

When next day Florus entered the papal apartment he found His Holiness lying on the carpet racked by convulsions. The poor boy tried in vain, like another Pygmalion, to warm the cold and fearful lips of his beloved. For fifteen days now Joanna remained in bed, hovering between life and death; and when after that long agony she rose at last from her bed she immediately went to Rome and locked herself in her private chapel, forbidding entry to everyone no less than to the sun's rays. There she was hounded day and night by sinister phantoms, like Saul after he saw Samuel's shadow. She would start up in a sweat at the creaking of a door, or faint if she heard an owl or a night-jar call from the roof of the Vatican. The sight of the inhabitants of heaven never has benefited the wretched mortals who were allowed to see visions. Selene was burned by the rays of Zeus, the holy Nikon was half-blinded by the radiance of the Virgin, St. Paul was blinded by the candescence of Jesus, and Zacharias was left dumb after the departure of the angel. The Hebrews in fact were so afraid of such visions that every night before sleeping they asked the All-Highest to guard them from things 'that walk by night.'

But while the Pontiff trembled before the inhabitants of the next world more powerful enemies began to menace his authority in this one while the wrath of the Romans increased against him daily. The Italians in those times were not like the peoples of constitutional nations today who regard kings as mere architectural ornaments adorning the political edifice, as statues, say, on the tops of temples. They were not very advanced in the knowledge of synonyms. They had not reached the point of being able to distinguish between the word 'reign' and the word 'govern.' They demanded that their leader rule, just as they demanded that their cooks should cook. Seeing the treasuries empty, the churches silent, the monasteries converted into taverns, the Saracens plundering the coasts and the brigands encamped in the suburbs of the sacred city, the poor Romans first questioned with atonishment, then with impatience, and finally with anger, what His Holiness could be doing with his time while so many enemies were afoot. Was he allowing his sword to rust in its sheath? The devout complained because no more benedictions were conferred on them, the beggars because their daily dole of lentils was not distributed, while the fanatics complained that for six whole months no sorcerer or heretic had been burned. As for the demoniacs, the lame and the paralytics, they wanted to know why the Pope had stopped working miracles. But by far the most incensed faction was made up of those priests who were dispossessed, the chancellors and custodians for whom there was no place at court, the parasites who had been turned out of the papal kitchens; and yet more vehement were the pimps and barbers who could not understand why they were excluded from the palace among whose recognised traditions had been shaving and womanising. All of them, having offered to everyone their devotions, talents, razors, and their clients, and foreseeing little to hope for, became firm revolutionaries. As they could no longer dip their horn-spoons in the papal broth they sought now to overturn the pot: like those Indians who cut down trees in order to eat their fruit.

Even nature that year seemed to have acquired something of a revolutionary disposition. The Tiber burst its banks and carried away fences, boats, towers and bridges in its course. Flowers forgot to bloom and cherries to ripen though it was already mid-May. The birds sat silent and dejected upon the boughs of the trees like the cocks of Jerusalem during Passion Week. But by far the most awful omens for the Romans were the clouds of locusts which fell in such quantities that for eight days they blotted out the rays of the sun while the thunder of their wings was like the noise of warlike chariots. These pests had six wings, eight feet, long hair like women and sharp stings like scorpions. I am not sure whether this description is strictly historical or whether the annalists stole it from the Apocalypse – on the principle of the evangelists who borrowed from the Old Testament to write the New.

At any rate these locusts were so voracious that after they had demolished the corn and the leaves on the trees they swarmed into the houses and even into the churches, where they ate the shew-bread on the altars and even the wax candles. Having eaten these they began to devour one another and fought in mid-air with so much ferocity that their dead bodies fell more thickly than hail in autumn. No Roman dared to stir out of his house without an umbrella or a helmet. This final plague brought the simmering anger of the faithful to the boil; it began to swell like the flood-waters of a river. Certain that the least sign from the Pontiff would disperse these winged monsters, they asked one another in desperation why Christ's representative kept his hands folded in his cassock and left his subjects to the mercy of the locusts. Naturally those estimable gentlemen who were firmly entrenched in their opposition to the government were about as slow to scent the approaching storm as Arab thoroughbreds are to scent a spring in the desert. It was they who, when the uprising started, arranged the rabble into companies and groups, and led them shrieking and howling under the windows of the Vatican.

At the sight of the rebels the guard withdrew behind the barred gateways and the courtiers rushed to embrace the crucifixes and the altars as the Theban virgins embraced the idols of the Acropolis when the seven chiefs once brandished their spears outside the gates. Only Florus, who during this long period had been deprived of his friend, was happy that he at last had an excuse to get beyond the firmly barred door of the chapel before which he had paced, night and day. He crossed the threshold to discover Joanna seated upon a pew and staring, with the air of an Egyptian navelwatcher, at her distended abdomen from which was to come not the Holy Ghost but her own shameful offspring. She was persuaded with considerable difficulty to appear before her subjects and attempt to calm the storm. When the pale and far-away figure of the Pontiff was thrown upon the window, illuminated by a sunbeam which pierced the lowering cloud of locusts for a moment, many of the revolutionaries, overtaken by an involuntary respect, found themselves reverently bowing as the Roman standards are said to have bowed before Christ whenever he appeared at the court of Pilate. But there were many irreverent hands which still grasped stones and rotten fruit, and many a Pharisaical mouth uttered insults and blasphemies upon the representative of Jesus. As he spoke the Pontiff reached out his hand to silence them. He declared that next day, at the beginning of Rogation week, he would anathematise the locusts in an official litany; but that meanwhile he would pronounce an anathema against all those who did not immediately return home. The papal promise instantly dispersed the anxiety and calmed the anger of the Roman populace. Their clamour resembled the tempests of the Propontis which, says Aristotle, can be calmed by a few drops of oil.

Early on the following morning everybody was busy in the palace as usual. The priests laid out their embroidered stoles, the deacons polished their sacrificial plate, the grooms curried the mules and in the great square the multitude, which loved festivals, looked forward with much rubbing of hands to the ceremony which would follow. The Rogation Day litany was, as with most Christian ceremonies, a pagan legacy of those who had performed fertility rites in the fields, had danced and sung about the altars of Demeter and Bacchus while they asked a blessing on corn, vine and turnip. Their descendants now proposed to ask the same favour with the same ceremony in which only the names of Demeter and Bacchus had been replaced by those of the Virgin and St. Martino. Today, however, there was a double ceremony for the anathema against the locusts was to be pronounced first.

In that golden century of faith not only sinful human beings but all mischievous animals, such as rats, ravens, wild boars, worms, tape-worms and fleas were subject to the anathemas of the church if they so much as dared to eat green vegetables or disturb the sleep of the faithful. But the crowds and the seriousness of the locust plague provided ample excuse for the ceremony which had been planned for today, and no Christian of Rome or the outlying districts was going to miss it. They all came.

While the courtiers, merry and optimistic, crowded the long corridors of the Vatican, Joanna said a tearful good-bye to her lover. Our poor heroine had passed an anxious and sleepless night, sometimes sunk in profound thought, and at others frantically trying on Pontifical robes one after another to find which of them would best conceal her outlines. The fateful words of the angel rang in her ears. Its appearance had removed at one blow the whole structure of her philosophy so that she found herself remembering now the scales in which the Archangel Michael weighed the soul, the Devil with his taws, the cauldrons, the freezing ice, the snakes, harpoons, thumbscrews, tongs and other furniture of the medieval Hell.

Then she went over in her mind the various philosophical systems, like transmigration, the translation of souls to the moon, and found herself thinking about earthquakes, locusts, leprosy and plague, always coming back to the same stark conclusion: namely that God seemed not only to have filled this world with grief and agony, but the other too with a host of terrible devils. These and other questions did our heroine debate throughout the night. The greater part of them I must omit as I wish to end my story. If I were a poet I would have said that my Pegasus could smell the stable and was driving me willy nilly towards it; but as a pedestrian in prose surely I have even more right to hint that after such a long journey I have grown tired, and look forward to my stable – or rather the climax of my story.

The good Florus observing the pallor and anxiety of his mistress sought to hold her back in every way, entreating her with tears to postpone the service. But having once accepted the bitter cup Joanna had no option but to drink it to the dregs. And besides, she could not have escaped now if she wanted to. The crowds encamped under the papal window stamped impatiently; candles fluttered, bells pealed, incense began to rise in clouds from the censers. So it was that His Holiness the Pope placed the triple crown upon his head, took up his pastoral staff, and left the arms of his beloved, possessed by presentiments as black as those ravens which fluttered about the head of Gracchus on the day of his death.

When the ruler of the faithful appeared in the open space before the Vatican thousands of Romans were waiting for the litany, and as he rode to the church of St. John they formed in two ranks and followed the procession. The standard bearers came first carrying the crosses and the ikons of the tutelary saints. After came the archdeacons in purple robes, followed by the barefooted abbots and friars, bending their ash-besprinkled heads to the ground. Under the standard of St. Marcellinus came the nuns and deaconesses, followed by the married women under the banner of St. Euphemia. Last of all came the young virgins dressed in white with their hair loose. They were sad because the locusts had left neither roses nor narcissi which they were accustomed, during those ages of faith, to wear in their hair and at their breasts. The lesser clergy, soldiery and the mob brought up the rear, and with them marched a rabble of hot-drink sellers and tavern-keepers who warmed the devotion of the faithful with beer, mead and concoctions made from quinces. This part of the crowd howled hymns to Jesus and St. Peter, but as there were some newly converted Saracens, German, Benedictines and Greek monks among it, not to mention a sprinkling of British theologians and others: and as each insisted on singing the psalms in their mother tongue, the cacophony may well be imagined. It was what the pious Chateaubriand might have described as a 'harmonious symphony of all nations honouring the Christ.'

The procession passed the Arch of Trajan and the Flavian amphitheatre and pressed on until it reached the Lateran Square. So overpowering was the heat and the dust, according to the chroniclers, that the Devil himself might have welcomed a dip in the holy water stoup. The swarms of struggling locusts flew above them, the bodies of the wounded falling to the ground, to

147

be trampled by the feet of the worshippers and the pack mules. All these circumstances increased the despondency and pain of the unhappy Joanna, who could by now hardly hold herself upright upon the back of her mule so acute had the pain in her stomach become. She stumbled twice as she ascended the steps of the magnificent throne from which she was to hurl anathemas upon the hordes of invading locusts.

Her Beatitude, after blessing and dipping the holy sprinkler in water, shook it to the East, West, South and North; then taking up a carved ivory crucifix she raised it up and made the sign of the cross at that pestilential cloud of struggling locusts. But all of a sudden the cross slipped from her fingers and was broken in pieces, and not long afterwards the Pontiff himself fell down, pale as death, on the steps of the throne. At this sight the faithful surged anxiously up, jostling together like sheep that a wolf has frightened. The archdeacons who carried His Holiness's train sprang forward to help him to his feet. But he lay there groaning and writhing, like a snake that has been cut in half. Now the whisper went up that His Beatitude had inadvertently trodden upon a mandrake root, or been stung by a scorpion or had eaten some poisonous mushrooms. But several in the crowd persisted that he was possessed of a devil and the Bishop of Porto, by far the greatest exorcist of the age, hurried forward to sprinkle holy water upon Joanna, who was by this time in labour, and to command the evil spirit to choose another dwelling place.

The crowd fixed its eyes upon the pallid face of the Pontiff, expecting to see the unclean spirit suddenly rush out of her mouth or ear; they were hardly prepared for what really happened. Great was the consternation when a premature infant was produced from among the voluminous folds of the papal vestments. The attending archdeacons recoiled in horror while the great circle of worshippers pressed in even closer, screaming and crossing themselves. Women climbed on the backs of their menfolk for a better view, while those already mounted on horses and mules stood in the saddle until the deacons were forced to use their standards and crucifixes as clubs to hew a passage through the mob.

Some hierarchs who were profoundly devoted to the Holy See sought to save the situation and change horror and disgust to amazement by crying out 'A miracle! A miracle!' They bellowed loudly calling the faithful to kneel and worship. But in vain. Such a miracle was unheard of; and indeed would have been a singular contribution to the annals of Christian thaumaturgy which, while it borrowed many a prodigy from the pagans, had not yet reached the point where it could represent any male saint as pregnant and bringing forth a child. So the roars of the pious were engulfed in the swelling thunder of the mob which began to kick and trample both the poor Papissa and her Papidion, shrieking out that they must be thrown into the Tiber. Florus managed to burst through the ring and take the unhappy Joanna in his arms. Her pallor had become deathly as now, raising her dying eyes to the sky, perhaps to remind Him who inhabits it, that she had emptied the cup to the last drop, she gave up the ghost murmuring with Isaiah: 'My face I gave for strokes, as a shame and a rebuke.'

No sooner had the sinful soul abandoned its temporal dwelling than a horde of devils rushed up from Hell to claim it, for they had long ago written it down in their catalogues as an unquestioned pledge; but at the same moment a phalanx of angels swept down from Heaven and repulsed them, insisting that her repentance had cancelled any rights the devils may have had upon her soul.

But the devils were disinclined to be persuaded and decided to contest the matter with their horns against the swords and arguments of the angels. The scuffle was quite a brisk one. Their weapons rang out like the collision of clouds and a rain of blood poured down upon the faithful in the great square. All at once the angel which had appeared to Joanna broke the ranks of the disputants and snatched up her unhappy soul which it carried off with it to – Purgatory probably. These miracles, dear reader, are not assembled from accounts given by four fishermen but by over four hundred venerated and habited chroniclers; in the presence of such an assembly of august witnesses we can only bow our heads and exclaim with Tertullian: 'I believe these things because they are unbelievable.'

The body of the lovely Joanna was buried on the spot where she fell. Her grave bore a marble relief depicting a woman bringing forth a baby. Florus became a hermit; and the pious pilgrims, in order not to contaminate their sandals by walking in the footsteps of the sacrilegious woman Pope, have ever since taken another road to the Lateran.

Notes

1 John Scotus Erigena. The eminent schoolman. d. 886.

2 I have been unable to trace any reference to a forger of this name.

3 St. Gutlhac was presbyter and hermit of Crowland, a desolate island off the Lincolnshire coast. Born a noble he distinguished himself in many a foray against the British. At the age of twenty-four however he retired from active life to Crowland where his piety at length attracted many admirers. His solitude was much troubled by carnal visions but he triumphed over them.

4 Garryon. The ancient name of the city of Yarmouth says a note by the author.

5 Eboracum. The ancient name of the city of York says a note by the author.

6 Alcuin. (Albinus) Born at York circa 735 where he received a monastic education. Encountering Charlemagne at Pavia in 782 he was invited to assume many posts of great political and ecclesiastical responsibility. One of these involved him with the education of Frankish nobles' sons.

7 Charlemagne.

8 Thor, Wotan, Erminsul, etc. Saxon deities worshipped in Westphalia. Charlemagne is reported to have overthrown the great idol to Erminsul and to have built a Christian chapel on the site of the temple.

9 I can find no trace of St. Paternus in Butler's *Lives* or any reference in Platina. His powers the reader will be able to guess from the context.

10 Criezoti. In modern Greek folk-lore.

11 Lit. 'Peda' or 'jump.'

12 St. Lioba. A good deal of the colouring matter in the first part of *Papissa Joanna* may be traced to the accounts given of the life of Boniface, the 'Apostle of Germany.' Born near Exeter in circa 680, he was a Saxon by birth. He was already famous when he left England in 716 to join the missionary Willibrord in Friesland. He found great favour with Pope Gregory II and later became primate of

Germany. He was responsible for several waves of Anglo-Saxon preachers descending upon his territory of operations, and among his Anglo-Saxon recruits were St. Willibald, St. Wigbert, St. Lioba and St. Thecla. He is also said to have founded the monastery of Fulda which features in this romance and to have died there. St. Willibald wrote his life. See Butler's *Lives of the Saints* and the Schaff-Herzog *Encyclopaedia of Religious Knowledge*.

13 St. Pachomius. A younger contemporary of St. Anthony and the real founder of the monastic life upon an island in the Nile. The author here puns upon the word 'paximadi' which means a very dry kind of biscuit-bread.

14 There are several Benedicts. Probably Benedict of Nursia, b. 480. He lived for three years at the bottom of a dismal cavern and had his food lowered to him on a rope by a colleague. On being discovered by some shepherds his appearance caused much alarm. Elected Abbot of Vicovaro in 510 he so far relaxed the severity of his habits as to permit his flock wine at meals.

15 Rabanus the Black (Rabanus Maurus), b. 776 and died 856. Brought up under the tutelage of Alcuin he became Abbot of Fulda in 822.

16 St. Genevieve, St. Francis, St. Libania, St. Luitberga. The author's sources are not stated; and his editor's resources have been all but exhausted in an attempt to track down saints with these names and habits. St. Genevieve is probably the patron Saint of Paris. She ate only on Sundays and Thursdays, and, says Butler, 'her prayer was almost continual and generally attended by a large flow of tears.' She saved Paris during an attack by Attila whose forces were repulsed by her prayers. St. Francis is possibly he of Paula who entered a monastery at the age of twelve and was among the most precocious of ascetics. In the matter of fasting particularly he was a virtuoso. St. Libania may possibly be St. Lebuin; while St. Luitberga, though she commands respect, cannot be traced among the authorities available at the time of writing.

17 St. Thecla, St. Margaret, St. Eugenia, St. Matrona. The first of these, though not recorded as the sister of St. Paul, is said to have accompanied him on several apostolic missions. Described in Butler as a girl of sweetness and intelligence and well-versed in profane literature, she early felt the call of God, and broke off her

engagement with a young man, whose despair turned to hatred. He denounced her to the authorities and she was condemned to be torn to pieces by wild animals. Placed in the lion-pit naked she caused such a sensation by her calm that even the lions recoiled from her; and when goaded on by their keepers could only be persuaded to lick her feet. Saved by this act of faith she lived to a ripe old age. In the case of Margaret it is not clear whether our author refers to the one who withstood the blandishments of the Governor of Antioch or to St. Margaret of Cortona. The first Margaret withstood both the Governor and the dragon which subsequently visited her while in close confinement at the Governor's orders; she waved a crucifix at the dragon which, say some authorities, burst into flames. She is the patron saint of Lyme Regis. As for St. Margaret of Cortona, 'The harshness of a stepmother and her own indulged propension to vice cast her headlong into the greatest disorders. The sight of the carcass of a man, half-putrefied, who had been her gallant, struck her with so great a fear of divine judgment that she in a moment became a perfect penitent. . . .' The account in Butler's *Lives of the Saints* continues: 'The austerities with which she punished her criminal flesh soon disfigured her body.' Then there is also Margaret 'The Pelogian,' perhaps the most likely. She is mentioned in *The Golden Legend*. She left home on her marriage day and retired to a convent. Eugenia was a daughter of Philip, Prefect of Alexandria. She passed many years as a monk and was ultimately made abbot. Her deception remained complete until one day, on being accused of dishonouring a virgin she uncovered her breasts as an irresistible proof of her innocence.

18 P. Soutsos who appears more than once in this romance was a milk-and-water poet of Athens, a contemporary of the author.

19 Platina in his *Life of Leo IV* says: 'He by diligence found out the bodies of the *sancti quatuor coronati* and built a church to them after a magnificent manner; and reposited their bodies under the altar, viz., Sempronianus, Claudius, Nicostratus, Castorius; to which he added those of Severus, Severianus, Carpoforus Victorinus, Marius . . . and Marcellinus. . .

20 St. Mary of Egypt was a prostitute before she became a Saint; the author is probably thinking of her confession in which he states

that she joined a band of pilgrims going to Jerusalem in order to exercise her profession.

21 St. Sergius, St. Febronia. Gibbons mentions a saint of Antioch called Sergius. Several saints and martyrs of the Roman Catholic Church bear this name. St. Febronia was an early Christian martyr.

22 St. Babylas and St. Prisca. St. Babylas was the most celebrated of the ancient bishops of Antioch and was put to death in Caesaria. St. Prisca may be the wife of Diocletian put to death by Licinius. She is mentioned in Gibbon.

23 Basil the Great. Born at Caesaria about 330 and died there 379.

24 St. Vitus' Dance, once widely prevalent in Germany and the Low Countries, was so called from the supposed power of St. Vitus over nervous and hysterical affections. St. Vitus was a native of Sicily. His nurse Crescentia and her husband Modestus shared his martyrdom in Lucania.

25 Lake Kopais near Athens.

26 The historians name him either Louis the Pious or Louis the Débonnaire, says a note by the author.

27 A reference to the guarantee of Greek Independence given by France, England and Russia.

28 Agobard. He was born in Spain in 779 and from 816 was Archbishop of Lyons. He was one of that group of great men who grew up in France under the influence of Charlemagne. He attacked and refuted many of the common superstitions of his day, among them the attributing of hailstorms to the machinations of sorcerers.

29 Theophilus Kairis. A modern Greek writer (1784–1852) whose writings earned him excommunication. After death his body was refused Christian burial.

30 Caesarius of Arles. Succeeded to the episcopal chair of Arles in 502. He was a great reformer and disciplinarian. Perhaps the greatest influence he exercised was with his *Regulae Duoe, altera ad Monarchos, altera ad Virgines*, which were often adopted by founders of monastic institutions before the rules of St. Benedict came into use. See the Schaff-Herzog *Encyclopaedia*.

31 A play upon the words 'Parthenotrophea' – schools for girl-

education: and 'Parthenopthoroea' – schools for girl-corruption. St. Peter Damien was a great reformer born in 998 in Ravenna.

32 St. Anna, mother of the Holy Virgin according to the tradition of the ancient church. In the eighth century Pope Leo III had the history of St. Joachim and Saint Anna painted on the basilica of San Paolo. The idea of immaculate conception was applied to her, but much later.

33 The ikon of the Virgin of Tinos is still as efficient as it ever was and large crowds gather for each celebration in August, coming from all over Greece and Asia Minor. Many authenticated cures have been placed to the credit of the ikon.

34 Theodora II was the wife of Theophilus (829–842). Says Gibbon: 'The character of Theophilus is a rare example in which religious zeal has allowed, and perhaps magnified, the virtues of an heretic and a persecutor. His valour was often felt by the enemies, and his justice by the subjects, of the monarchy; but the valour of Theophilus was rash and fruitless and his justice arbitrary and cruel.' Theophilus was a bitter iconoclast and the cruelty with which he enforced his measures against image-worship produced great bitterness in the monasteries whose monks chiefly lived by the manufacture of holy images. Theodora, however, was an ardent image-worshipper. On his death she reversed his laws and called back all those image-worshippers whom Theophilus had banished. In 842 she convened a synod in Constantinople which restored the images to the churches throughout her realms. For details of this fascinating theological war see Tozer's *History of the Eastern Church*.

35 Nestorious became bishop of Constantinople in 428. He regarded the pet epithet of the Alexandrian teachers 'Theotokos' or 'Mother of God' as a heathenish mixture of divine and earthly. 'Has God a mother? The creature has not borne Him who is uncreate.' Not God the Logos but only the human nature, had a mother. These speculations of Nestorius shook Constantinople. For an accurate account of these theological wars see Tozer's *Eastern Church*.

36 The 'asterisk' is a star-shaped ornament used in the Greek church to cover the chalice during the Liturgy and on which the linen veil is afterwards placed to encircle the chalice.

37 The author probably took this gallery of ascetics direct from the *Lives of the Fathers.*

38 Acorn. A note by the author says that this drink is mentioned in Athenaios I. 62.

39 First Council of Nice or Nicea in Asia Minor was held in 325.

40 A friendly attempt to involve Joanna in the theological conflicts of the day. In a previous note it will be seen that the venerable Nestorius had complained about the use of the word 'Theotokos' for the Mother of God. She could, he averred, be with propriety called 'Christotokos' or 'Christ-bearing' but not 'Theotokos.' Joanna seems to be taking a leaf out of his book in this passage. 'Ootokos' means 'egg-bearing' and 'zootokos' means 'child-bearing' – both epithets calculated to confuse the argument. Joanna's attitude to theology is highly irreverent.

41 Born in Alexandria in the fourth century and famous for her learning. She was cut to pieces by a Christian mob.

42 Copronymous. So called because he fouled the baptismal font. Gibbon gives the following portrait of him. 'In a long reign of thirty-four years, the son and successor of Leo, Constantine the Fifth, Surnamed Copronymous, attacked with less temperate zeal the images or idols of the church. Their votaries have exhausted the bitterness of religious gall in their portrait of this spotted panther, this antichrist, this flying dragon of the serpent's seed, who surpassed the vices of Elagabalus and Nero. His reign was a long butchery of whatever was most noble, or holy, or innocent, in his empire. In person, the emperor assisted at the execution of his victims, surveyed their agonies, listened to their groans, and indulged, without satiating, his appetite for blood; a plate of noses was accepted as a grateful offering and his domestics were often scourged and mutilated by the royal hand. His surname was derived from the pollution of his baptismal font. The infant might be excused, but the manly pleasures of Copronymous degraded him below the level of the brute; his lust confounded the external distinctions of sex and species; and he seemed to extract some unnatural delight from the objects most offensive to human sense. In his religion, the Iconoclast was an Heretic, a Jew, a Mahometan, a Pagan, and an Atheist. His life was stained with the most opposite

vices, and the ulcers which covered his body anticipated before his death the sentiment of hell-tortures. . . .' In justice to Copronymous it should be added that the passage continues. 'Of these accusations, which I have so patiently copied, a part is refuted by its own absurdity; and in the private anecdotes of the life of princes, the lie is more easy as the detection is more difficult.'

43 The word 'tympanitikos' is used for a werwolf or vampire. The belief is that the body of a vampire, when dug up, will not only appear to be alive but will have assumed a drum-like and distended shape.

44 A note by the author says: 'The monastery of Daphni was indeed taken over by the Benedictines in the time of the dukes of Larochus whose grave may be seen at the entrance to the church.' I have not verified this statement.

45 A note by the author says: 'Regarding the various orders see the explanations of Leo Allatius and the "Confessionali" of Nicodemus.'

46 A note by the author says: 'This phrase I have borrowed from Samphortius.'

47 Leo IV. 847–855. Platina says: 'He was a person of so much prudence and courage that, as the Gospel directs, he could, when it was necessary, imitate either the wisdom of the serpent or the innocence of the dove.'

48 Sergius. 844–847, was a Roman. Platina says that he was surnamed Bocca di Porco or Pigmouth, which for very shame he changed to Servius.

49 See note 19 on Leo IV, by Platina, who does not, however, record the other miracles. They are probably culled from Baronius or Muratori.

50 A note by the author says: 'This description was taken from Baronius.'

51 See Platina for an account of the extraordinary natural phenomena accompanying the election or death of Popes; plagues of locusts, storms of blood, etc. The author is probably thinking of them in this passage.

Shorter Bibliography

POPE JOAN, THE FEMALE POPE. An historical study translated from the Greek. With a preface by C. H. Collette. G. Redway: London, 1886.

LA PAPESSE JEANNE, roman historique. Précédé d'une importante étude historique. Ouvrage traduit du grec moderne. Paris, 1878. (Part of the *Bibliothèque moderne*.)

POPE JOAN: an historical romance. Translated (and abridged) by J. H. Freese. 1900.

LA PAPESSE JEANNE . . . Septième édition revue et augmentée d'une étude critique par J. Barbey d'Aurevilly, etc. Paris, 1881.

LA PAPESSE JEANNE. Roman médiéval. Traduit du grec par A. Jarry et J. Saltas. Paris, 1908.

See Buet (C.) Études historiques. LA PAPESSE JEANNE. Réponse à M. E. Rhoïdis. 1878.